It was near—it was almost upon them. It hovered, monstrous and glowing in the mouth of the tunnel, filling the high black circle of its disc. . . .

And then, with one great swoop, it burst into the violet daylight of Carcasilla.

Alan's confused impressions of the thing were too contradictory to have meaning. Was it monstrously tall? He could not tell, even as it stood there against the black mouth of the disc. Had it been blazingly robed in light against that blackness? He couldn't be sure.

Alan could not stir—he could only stand and stare, drowning in helpless wonder as he watched. This was the creature that sought him since he had come to Carcasilla, this was the nameless creature that had haunted all his waking and sleeping hours.

The great, striding god went through the crowd of Carcasillians like a reaper through grain, snatching up, enveloping, hurling aside figure after figure . . . flashing closer with each moment.

And then the towering inhuman thing stooped above his head with an avid swoop, its robes falling about him like blindness to shut out the violet day. It had been starving for countless centuries, and it had found him. . . .

EARTH'S LAST CITADEL

C. L. Moore and Henry Kuttner

ace books
A Division of Charter Communications Inc.
A GROSSET & DUNLAP COMPANY
1120 Avenue of the Americas
New York, New York 10036

EARTH'S LAST CITADEL

Copyright, 1943, by Popular Publications, Inc.

All rights reserved. No part of this book may be reproduced in any form or by any means, except for the inclusion of brief quotations in a review, without permission in writing from the publisher.

All characters in this book are fictitious. Any resemblance to actual persons, living or dead, is purely coincidental.

An ACE Book

Printed in U.S.A.

Other Titles in the ACE Great Years Series:

ALIEN PLANET, Pratt

ARMAGEDDON 2419 A.D., Nowlan

THE BLIND SPOT

THE BRAIN-STEALERS

A BRAND NEW WORLD, Cummings

THE GALAXY PRIMES, Smith

INTERPLANETARY HUNTER, Barnes

METROPOLIS, von Harbou

THE MIGHTIEST MACHINE, Campbell

THE MOON IS HELL, Campbell

THE RADIO BEASTS

THE RADIO PLANET

SCIENCE FICTION: THE GREAT YEARS VOL I, Pohl

SCIENCE FICTION: THE GREAT YEARS VOL II, Pohl

SENTINELS FROM SPACE

THE ULTIMATE WEAPON, Campbell

EARTH'S
LAST
CITADEL

PROLOGUE

BEHIND THE LOW ridge of rock to the north was the Mediterranean. Alan Drake could hear it and smell it. The bitter chill of the North African night cut through his torn uniform, but sporadic flares of whiteness from the sea battle seemed to give him warmth, somehow. Out there the big guns were blasting, the battlewagons thundering their fury.

This was it.

And he wasn't in it—not this time. His job was to bring Sir Colin safely out of the Tunisian desert. That, it seemed, was important.

Squatting in the cold sand, Alan ignored the Scots scientist huddled beside him, to stare at the ridge as though his gaze could hurdle its summit and leap out to where the ships were fighting. Behind him, from the south, came the deep echoing noise of heavy artillery. That, he knew, was one jaw of the trap that was closing on him. The tides of war changed so swiftly—there was nothing for them now but heading blindly for the Mediterranean and safety.

He had got Sir Colin out of one Nazi trap already, two

breathless days ago. But Colin Douglas was too valuable a man for either side to forget easily. And the Nazis would be following. They were between the lines now, lost, trying desperately to reach safety and stay hidden.

Somewhere in the night sky a nearing plane droned high. Moonlight glinted on Drake's smooth blond head as he leaped for the shadow of a dune, signaling Sir Colin fiercely. Drake crouched askew, favoring his left side where a bullet gouge ran aslant up one powerful forearm and disappeared under his torn sleeve. He'd got that two nights ago in the Nazi raid, when he snatched Sir Colin away barely in time.

Army Intelligence meant such work, very often. Drake was a good man for his job, which was dangerous. A glance at his tight-lipped poker-face would have told that. It was a face of curious contrasts. Opponents were at a loss trying to gauge his character by one contradictory feature or the other; more often than not they guessed wrong.

The plane's droning roar was very near now. It shook the whole sky with a canopy of sound. Sir Colin said impersonally, huddled against the dune:

"That meteor we saw last night—must have fallen near here, eh?"

There were stories about Sir Colin. His mind was a great one, but until the war he had detested having to use it. Science was only his avocation. He preferred the pleasures which food and liquor and society supplied. A decadent Epicurus with an Einstein brain—strange combination. And yet his technical skill—he was a top-rank physicist—had been of enormous value to the Allies.

"Meteor?" Drake said. "I'm not worried about that.

But the plane—" He glanced up futilely. The plane was drawing farther away. "If they spotted us. . . ."

Sir Colin scratched himself shamelessly. "I could do with a plane now. There seemed to be fleas in Tunisia—carnivorous sand-fleas, be damned to them."

"You'd better worry about that plane—and what's in it."

Sir Colin glanced up thoughtfully. "What?"

"A dollar to a sand-flea it's Karen Martin."

"Oh." Sir Colin grimaced. "Her again. Maybe this time we'll meet."

"She's a bad egg, Sir Colin. If she's really after us, we're in for trouble."

The big Scotsman grunted. "An Amazon, eh?"

"You'd be surprised. She's damned clever. She and her sidekick draw good pay from the Nazis, and earn it, too. You know Mike Smith?"

"An American?" Sir Colin scratched again.

"Americanized German. He's got a bad history, too. Racketeer, I think, until Repeal. When the Nazis got going, he headed back for Germany. Killing's his profession, and their routine suits him. He and Karen make a really dangerous team."

The Scotsman got laboriously to his feet, looking after the vanished plane.

"Well," he said, "if that was the team, they'll be back."

"And we'd better not be here." Drake scrambled up, nursing his arm.

The Scotsman shrugged and jerked his thumb forward. Drake grinned. His blue eyes, almost black under the shadow of the full lids, held expressionless impassivity. Even when he smiled, as he did now, the eyes did not change.

"Come on," he said.

The sand was cold; night made it pale as snow in the faint moonlight. Guns were still clamoring as the two men moved toward the ridge. Beyond it lay the Mediterranean and, perhaps, safety.

Beyond it lay—something else.

In the cup that sloped down softly to the darkened sea was—a crater. A shimmering glow lay half-buried in the up-splashed earth. Ovoid-shaped, that glow. Its mass was like a monstrous radiant coal in the dimness.

For a long moment the two men stood silent. Then, "Meteor?" Drake asked.

There was incredulity in the scientist's voice. "It can't be a meteor. They're never that regular. The atmosphere heated it to incandescence, but see—the surface isn't even pitted. If this weren't war I'd almost think it was"—he brought out the words after a perceptible pause—"some kind of manmade ship from—"

Drake was conscious of a strange excitement. "You mean, more likely it's some Axis super-tank?"

Sir Colin didn't answer. Caution forgotten, he had started hastily down the slope. There was a faint droning in the air now. Drake could not be sure if it was a returning plane, or if it came from the great globe itself. He followed the Scotsman, but more warily.

It was very quiet here in the valley. Even the shore birds must have been frightened away. The sea-battle had moved eastward; only a breeze stirred through the sparse bushes with a murmur of leaves. A glow rippled and darkened and ran like flame over the red-hot metal above them when the wind played upon those smooth, high surfaces. The air still had an oddly scorched smell.

The night silence in the valley had been so deep that when Drake heard the first faint crackling in the scrubby desert brush he found that he had whirled, gun ready, without realizing it.

"Don't shoot," a girl's light voice said from the darkness. "Weren't you expecting me?"

Drake kept his pistol raised. There was an annoying coldness in the pit of his stomach. Sir Colin, he saw, from the corner of his eye, had stepped back into the dark.

"Karen Martin, isn't it?" Drake said. And his skin crawled with the expectation of a bullet from the night shadows. It was Sir Colin they wanted alive, not himself.

A low laugh in the dark, and a slim, pale figure took shape in the wavering glow from the meteor. "Right. What luck, our meeting like this!"

Underbrush crashed behind her and another shape emerged from the bushes. But Drake was watching Karen. He had met her before, and he had no illusions about the girl. He remembered how she had fought her way up in Europe, using slyness, using trickery, using ruthlessness as a man would use his fists. The new Germany had liked that unscrupulousness, needed it—used it. All the better that it came packaged in slim, curved flesh, bronze-curled, blue-eyed, with shadowy dimples and a mouth like red velvet, the unstable brilliance of many mixed races shining in her eyes.

Drake was scowling, finger motionless on the gun-trigger. He was, he knew, in a bad spot just now, silhouetted against the brilliance of the—the thing from the sky. But Sir Colin was still hidden, and he had a gun.

"Mike," Karen said, "you haven't met Alan Drake. Army Intelligence—American."

A deep, lazy voice from beyond the girl said, "Better drop the gun, buddy. You're a good target."

Drake hesitated. There was no sign from Sir Colin. That meant,—what? Karen and Mike Smith were probably not alone. Others might be following, and swift action should be in order.

He saw Karen's eyes lifting past him to the glowing surface above. In its red reflection her face was very curious. Her voice, irritating sure of itself, carried on the ironic pretense of politeness.

"What have we here?" she inquired lightly. "Not a tank? The High Command will be interested—" She stepped aside for a better look.

Drake said dryly, "Maybe it's a ship from outer space. Maybe there's something inside—"

There was.

The astonishing certainty of that suddenly filled his mind, stilling all other thought. For an incredible instant the moonlit valley wavered around him as a probing and a questioning fumbled through his brain.

Karen took two uncertain backward steps, the self-confidence wiped off her face by blank amazement, as if the questioning had invaded her mind too. Behind her Mike Smith swore abruptly in a bewildered undertone. The air seemed to quiver through the Mediterranean valley, as if an inconceivable Presence had suddenly brimmed it from wall to wall.

Then Sir Colin's voice spoke from the dark. "Drop your guns, you two. Quick. I can—"

His voice died. Suddenly, silently, without warning, the valley all around them sprang into brilliant light. Time stopped for a moment, and Drake across Karen's red head could see Mike hesitate with lifted gun, see the gangling Sir Colin tense a dozen feet beyond, see every leaf and twig in the underbrush with unbearable distinctness.

Then the light sank. The glare that had sprung out from the great globe withdrew inward, like a tangible thing, and a smooth, soft, blinding darkness followed after.

When sight returned to them, the globe was a great pale moon resting upon its crest of up-splashed earth. All heat and color had gone from it in the one burst of cool brilliance, and it rested now like a tremendous golden bubble in the center of the valley.

A door was opening slowly in the curve of the golden hull.

Drake did not know that his gun-arm was dropping, that he was turning, moving forward toward the ship with slow-paced steps.

He was not even aware of the others crackling through the brush beside him toward that dark doorway.

Briefly their reflections swam distorted in the golden curve of the hull. One by one they bent their heads under the low lintel of that doorway, in silence, without protest.

The darkness closed around them all.

Afterward, for a while, the great moon-globe lay quiet, shedding its radiance. Nothing stirred but the wind.

Later an almost imperceptible quiver shook the reflections in the curved surfaces of the ship. The crest of earth that splashed like a wave against the sphere washed higher, higher. As smoothly as if through water, the ship was sinking into the sand of the desert. The ship was large, but the sinking did not take very long.

Shortly before dawn armed men on camels came riding over the ridge. But by then earth had closed like water over the ship from space.

I

THE CITADEL

It seemed to Alan Drake that he had been rocking here forever upon the ebb and flow of deep, intangible tides. He stared into grayness that swam as formlessly as his swimming mind, and eternity lay just beyond it. He was quite content to lie still here, rocking upon the long, slow ages.

Reluctantly, after a long while, he decided that it was no longer infinity. By degrees the world came slowly into focus—a vast curve of a dim and glowing hollow rounded out before his eyes, mirrory metal walls, a ceiling shining and golden, far above. The rocking motion was imperceptibly ceasing, too. Time no longer cradled him upon its ebb and flow. He blinked across the vast hollow while memory stirred painfully. It was quiet as death in here; but he should not be alone.

Karen lay a little way from him, her red hair showering across the bent arm pillowing her head. With a slow, impersonal pleasure he liked the way the curved lines of her caught shadow and low light as she sprawled there asleep.

He sat up very slowly, very stiffly, like an old man. Memory was returning—there should be others. He saw them in a moment, relaxed figures dreaming on the shining floor.

And beyond them all, in the center of the huge sphere, was the high, dark doorway, narrow and pointed at the top like an arrow, within which blackness would be lying curdled into faintly visible clouds of deeper and lesser darkness. That was the Alien. The name came painfully into his brain, and his stiff lips moved soundlessly, forming it. He remembered—what did he remember? It was all so long ago it really couldn't matter much now, anyhow. He thought of the slow-swinging years upon which he had rocked so long.

He frowned. Now how did he know it had been Time that rocked him in his sleep? Why was he so sure that years had ebbed like water through the darkness of this mirrory place and the silence of his dreams? Dreams! That must be it! He had dreamed—about the Alien, for instance. He had not known that name when he fell asleep. His mind was beginning to thaw a bit, and now there was a sharp distinction in it between the things that had happened before this sleep came upon him—and afterward.

Afterward, in the long interval between sleeping and waking, the Alien was a part of that afterward. The things he dimly knew about it must have come floating into his mind from somewhere entirely outside the past he remembered. He closed his eyes and struggled hard to recall those dreams.

No use. He shook his head dizzily. The memories swam formlessly just out of conscious reach. Later, they might come back—not now. He stretched, feeling the long muscles slip pleasantly along his shoulders. In a moment or two the others would be waking.

It would be wiser if they woke unarmed. Whatever had been happening here in the dim time while Alan slept, Karen and Smith would wake enemies still. From here he could see that a revolver lay on the shining floor under Karen's hand. He got up stiffly, conscious of an overwhelming lassitude, and leaned to take the gun from her relaxed fingers.

Above her as he straightened he saw the high, arched doorway, and a sudden shock jolted him. For that dark and narrow portal was untenanted now. Nothing moved there, no curdled darkness, no swirl of black against black. The Alien was gone.

Why he was so certain, he did not know. No power on earth, he thought, could have drawn him to that arrow-shaped doorway to peer inside. But without it, he still knew they were alone now in the great empty shell of the ship.

He knew they had all come in here, out of the desert night and the distant thunder of sea-fighting—come in silence and obedience to a command not theirs to question. They had slept. And in their sleeping, dreamed strangely. The Alien, hovering in the darkness of its doorway, must have controlled those dreams. And now the Alien had gone. Where, why, when?

Karen stirred in her sleep. The dreams were still moving through her brain, perhaps; perhaps she might remember when she woke, as he had not. But she would remember, too, that they were enemies. Alan Drake's mind flashed back to the urgent present, and he stepped over her, past Sir Colin, to Mike Smith. He was lying on his side with a hand thrust under his coat as if even in the mindless lassitude which had attended their coming here, he had reached for his weapon.

Mike Smith groaned a little as Alan rolled him over, searching for and finding a second gun. An instinctive antagonism flared in Alan as he looked down upon the big, bronzed animal at his feet. Mike Smith, soldier of fortune, had battled his way across continents to earn the reputation for which Nazi Germany paid him. A reputation for tigerish courage, for absolute ruthlessness. One glance at his blunt brown features told that.

Karen sat up shakily. For a full minute she stared with blind blue eyes straight before her. But then awareness suddenly flashed into them and she met Alan's gaze. Like a mask, wariness dropped over her face. Her finger closed swiftly, then opened to grope about the floor beside her. Simultaneously she glanced around for Mike.

Alan laughed. The sound was odd, harshly cracked, as if he had not used his throat-muscles for a long time.

"I've got the guns, Karen," he said. A distant ghost mocked him from the high vaults above them. *"Guns—Karen—guns—Karen. . . ."*

She glanced up and then back again, and he wondered if a little shudder ran over her. Did she remember? Did she share this inexplicable feeling of strange nameless loss, of wrongness and disaster beyond reason? She did not betray it.

Mike Smith was getting slowly to his feet, shaking his head like a big cat, groping for the guns that were not there. Deliberately Alan crossed to the curved wall. He wanted something solid at his back. Curiously, he noticed that his feet roused no echoes in all that vast, hollow place. Walking on steel as if he walked on velvet, he carried his load of guns toward the great circular crack in the outer wall that outlined the closed door they had entered through. Mike and Karen watched him dazedly. Beyond them, Sir Colin was sitting up, blinking.

Mike's eyes were on the gun that Alan held steadily. He said:

"Karen, what's up? Were we gassed?" And his voice was rusty too, unused.

Sir Colin's burred tones almost creaked as he spoke. Faint echoes roused among the shadows overhead. "Maybe we were," he said. "Maybe we were."

There was silence. Four people had dreamed the same dream, or a part of it. They were groping in their memories now, and finding no more than Alan had found to judge by their bewildered faces. Presently Karen shook her red head and said:

"I want my gun back."

Sir Colin was staring about, uneasily rubbing his beard. "Wait," he said. "Things have changed, you know."

"Things may have changed," the girl said, and took a step toward Alan. "But I still have my job to do."

"For Germany," Alan murmured, and gently covered the revolver's trigger with his middle finger. "Better stay where you are, Karen. I don't trust you."

Sir Colin's eyes were troubled under the shaggy reddish brows. I'm not so sure there is a Germany," he said bluntly. "There's—"

Alan saw the almost imperceptible signal Karen gave.

Mike Smith had apparently been paying little attention to the dialogue. But now, without an instant's warning, he flung himself forward in a long smooth leap toward Alan. No—to Alan's left. The revolver had swung in a little arc before Alan realized his mistake. He saw Karen coming at him and swept the gun in a vicious blow at her head.

He didn't want to kill her—merely to put her out of the picture so that he could attend to Smith. But Karen's movement had been startling swift. She slid under the swinging gun, twisted sidewise, and suddenly she had crashed into him with the full weight of her body, jolting him back hard against the closed port. Alan stumbled, and felt the door slip smoothly away. He swayed on his heels against empty air. Mike Smith was coming in, lithe and boneless as a big cat, a joyous little smile on his face.

Motion slowed down, then. For Alan, it always slowed down in moments like this, so that he could see everything at once and act with lightning deliberation. Hard ground crunched under his heels as he pivoted and put all his force into a smashing blow that caught Mike Smith heavily across the jaw with the gun-barrel.

Mike went back and down, teeth bared in a feline snarl. Alan took one long forward stride to finish the job—and then saw Karen. And what he saw froze him. She had paused in the doorway, and it was surely not a trick that had twisted her smooth features into such a look of blank astonishment. Behind her, Sir Colin stood frozen, too, the same incredulity on his face.

Drake turned slowly, still holding his gun ready. Then for a moment his mind went lax, and what he saw before him had no significance at all.

For this was not the flame-scorched valley they had left.

And it was not morning, or noon, or night. There was only a ruddy twilight here, and a flat unfeatured landscape across which patches of mist drifted aimlessly as they watched, like clouds before a sluggish wind. Low down in the sky hung a dull and ruddy sun that they could look upon unblinded, with steady eyes.

Briefly, in the distance, something moved high up across the sky. There was a dark shape out there somewhere, a building monstrously silhouetted against the sun. But the mists closed in like curtains to veil it from his gaze, as if it were a secret to this dead world not for living eyes to see.

Sir Colin was the first who came to life. He reached out a big, red-knuckled hand and barred Mike Smith's automatic lurch forward, toward Alan and the gun.

"Not now," he burred. "Not now! You can forget about Germany. And Bizerte and Sousse and all Tunisia too, all Africa. This is—"

Alan let his own gun sink. Their quarrel seemed curiously lacking in point now, somehow against the light from that dying sun. For Germany and America and England had been—must have been—dust for countless millenniums. Their way did not belong in a world from which all passion must have ebbed forever long ago.

How long?

"It's Time," Alan heard himself whisper. "Time —gone out like a tide and left us stranded."

In the silence Karen cried, "It's still a dream—it must be!" But her voice was hushed to a half-whisper by the desolation all around, and she let the words die. Alan shook his head. He knew. They all knew, really. That was part of the dream they shared. By tacit agreement none of them mentioned that cloudy interval that had passed between their sleeping and their waking, but in it enough had seeped into their minds to have no doubt there now. This was no shock, after the first surprise wore away.

"Look," Sir Colin said, stepping away from the ship. "Whatever happened, we must have been buried." He pointed to the mounds of sandy soil heaped around the great sphere, as if it had thrust itself up from the depths of the earth. And even the soil was dead. This upheaval from far underground had turned up no moisture, no richness, no life.

"We'd better have our guns again, all of us," Karen said in a flat voice. "We may need them."

Mike Smith returned his guns to their holsters beneath his coat, and laughed with a short, unpleasant bark. Alan turned an impassively icy gaze upon him. He knew why Mike laughed. Mike was making the mistake that many others had made when they saw Alan Drake smile. Mike thought it was the fear of the unknown world, not simple acceptance of altered conditions, which had made Alan give up the gun. Well, Mike would have to learn sooner or later that the gentleness of Alan's smile was not a sign of weakness.

"Listen!" called Karen breathlessly. "Didn't you hear it? Listen!"

And while they all stood in strained quiet, a far, faint keening cry from high overhead came floating down to them through the twilight and the mist. Not a bird-cry. They all heard it clearly, and they must all have known it came from a human throat. While they stood frozen, it sounded again, nearer and lower and infinitely sad. And then across their range of vision, high in the ruddy gloom, a slim, winged shape floated, riding the air-currents like a condor with broad, pale wings outspread. They had glimpsed it before. And it was no bird-form. Clearly, even at this distance, they all could see the contours of a human body sailing on winged arms high in the twilight.

Once more the infinitely plaintive, thin cry keened through the air before the thing suddenly beat its winged arms together and went soaring off into the dimness, with the echoes of its heart-breaking wail fading on the air behind it.

No one spoke. Every face was lifted to the chilly wind as the pale, soaring speck melted into the sky and vanished far out over the unfeatured landscape. Alan found himself wondering if this slim, winged thing fading into the twilight would be the last man on earth, down an unimaginable line of evolution that had left all humanity winged and wailing—and mindless.

Alan shook himself a little.

"Evolution," Sir Colin was murmuring, an echo of Alan's thought. "So that's the end of the race, is it? How long have we slept, then?"

"One thing," said Alan in as brisk a voice as he could manage. "Whatever the thing was, it's got to eat. Somewhere in the world there must be some food and water left."

"Good for you, laddie," Sir Colin grinned. "Hadn't thought of that yet. Maybe there's hope for us yet, if we follow—"

"Don't forget, it can fly," reminded Karen.

Alan shrugged. "All the more reason to start after it now, while we're fresh. There isn't anything here to stay for."

"I think I'll just have a wee look inside before we go," put in Sir Colin thoughtfully. "There's a bare chance. . . ." He led the way back inside, and the rest followed, none of them willing to stay out alone in the desert of the world.

But there was nothing here. Only the vast curved walls, the confused reflections of themselves that swam dizzily when they moved. Only empty concavity, and the arrow-shaped doorway behind which nothing dwelt now. The Alien was gone, but whether he—it—had just preceded them into the ruddy twilight of the world's end, or whether he had been gone for many years when they woke, there was no way of guessing.

"If this was a space-ship once," murmured Sir Colin, scratching his rusty beard, "there must have been controls, motors—something! Now where could they be but there?" And he cocked a bristling eyebrow toward the dark doorway.

A little coldness shivered through Alan and was gone. He did not know what he remembered of that narrow door, but the thought of approaching it made the flesh crawl on his bones.

Sir Colin moved as slowly toward the door as if he too shared the unreasoning revulsion, but he moved, and Alan followed at his heels. He was at Sir Colin's elbow when the hulking scientist stooped his big, bony shoulders forward to peer into that slitted doorway they all feared without remembering why.

"Um—dark," grunted the Scotsman. He was fumbling

in the pocket of his shapeless suit. He found a tiny flashlight there and clicked on an intense needle-beam of light that flared in blinding reflection from the wall as he swung it toward the doorway.

He grunted in astonishment. "It shouldn't work," he muttered. "A battery, after a million years—"

But it did work, and it was useless. The light, turned to the narrow doorway, seemed to strike a wall of darkness and spray backward. That black interior seemed as solidly tangible as brick. Sir Colin put out his gun-hand and saw it vanish to the wrist in dark like water. He jerked it out again, unharmed.

Alan whistled softly. There was a moment of silence.

"All the same," Alan said doggedly, "we've got to explore that room before we leave. There's just a bare hope of something in there that can help us."

He drew his own gun and took a deep breath, and stepped over the threshold of the arrow-shaped door like a man plunging into deep water. The most hideous revulsions crawled through every nerve of his body as that blinding darkness closed over his eyes. He could not even hear Sir Colin's step behind him, but he felt a groping hand find his shoulder and grip it, and the two men moved forward with wary, shuffling steps into a darkness that blinded every sense like oblivion itself.

Alan's outstretched hand found the wall. He followed it grimly, prepared for anything. He was trying very hard not to remember that once the Alien had seemed to brim this little room, filling the high doorway with a curling and shifting of dark against dark.

It was a small room. They groped their way around the

wall and, in a space of time that might or might not have been long, Alan felt the wall fall away beneath his fingers, and he stepped out into the comparative brightness of the great dim hollow again. He had a moment of utter vertigo. Then the floor steadied under his feet, and he was looking into Sir Colin's face, white and a little sick.

"You—you look the way I feel," he heard himself saying inanely. "Well—"

Sir Colin put his gun away methodically, pocketed the flash. "Nothing," he said, in a thinnish voice. "Nothing at all."

Karen lifted questioning blue eyes to them, searched each face in turn. She did not ask them what they had found inside the arrowy doorway, perhaps she did not want to know. But after a moment, in a subdued voice, she echoed Mike.

"Yes, we'd better go. This ship—it's no good any more. It will never move again." She said it flatly, and for a moment Alan almost recaptured the memory he had been groping for. She was right. This ship had never needed machinery, but whatever motive power had lifted it no longer existed. It was as dead as the world it had brought them to.

He followed the others toward the door.

The dust of the world's end rose in sluggish whirls around their feet, and settled again as they plodded across the desert. The empty sphere of the ship was hidden in the mists behind them. Nothing lay ahead but the invisible airy path the birdman had followed, and the hope of food and water somewhere before their strength gave out.

Alan scuffed through the dust which was all that remained of the vivid world he had left only yesterday, before the long night of his sleep. This dust was Tunis, it was the bazaars and the shouting Arabs of Bizerte. It was tanks and guns and great ships, his own friends, and the titanic battle that had raged about the Mediterranean. He shivered in the frigid wind that whirled the dust of ages around him. Iron desolation was all that remained, desolation and silence and—

There was that cryptic structure he had glimpsed, or thought he glimpsed, against the sky. It might hold life —if he had not imagined it. The bird-like creatures might have come from there. In any case, they might as well walk in that direction, lacking any other sign.

The stillness was like death around them. But was it stillness? Alan tilted his head away from the wind to catch that distant sound, then called out, "Wait!"

In a moment they heard it, too, the great rushing roar from so far away that its intensity was diminished to a whisper without, somehow, diminishing its volume. The roar grew louder. Now it was low thunder, shaking the drifting mists, shaking the very ground they stood on. But it did not come nearer. It went rushing and rumbling off into diminuendo again, far away through the mists.

They stood there blindly, huddled together against the immense mystery and menace of a force that could shake the earth as it passed. And while they still stood quiet a faint, thin cry from overhead electrified them all.

"The bird again!" Karen whispered, and with the nervous dig of her fingers into his, Alan realized suddenly that they had been clutching one another with tense hands.

"There it is!" cried Mike Smith suddenly. "I see it! Look!" And his gun was in his hand with magical smoothness and swiftness, lifting toward the pale winged figure that was sailing low through the thinning mists overhead.

Alan's leap was pure reflex, too swift for even his own reasoning to follow. He had no time to wonder why he did it, but he felt his muscles gather and release with coiled-spring violence, and then his hurtling shoulder struck solid flesh, and he heard Mike grunt hollowly. The next moment the ground received them both with jolting force.

Alan rolled over and got to his feet, automatically brushing himself off and frowning down at Mike, who lay motionless, his gun a foot away.

The basic difference between the two men had come clearly into sight in the moment when the bird-creature sailed across the sky. Mike's instant reaction was to kill, Alan's to prevent that slaughter.

Sir Colin hulked forward and picked up Mike's fallen gun.

Mike was up then, swiftly recovered, and poised. Karen stepped in front of his catlike rebound. "Wait," she said, putting out an arm that stopped him in midstride. "Drake's right. We don't know what the sound of a shot might bring down on us. And those bird-things—what do we know about them? They might be—property. And the owners might be even less human than they are."

"I just wanted to wing the thing," Mike snarled. "How the hell can we trail a bird? It might lead us to food if we'd got it down on the ground. That's sense."

"We mustn't make enemies before we know their strength," Karen told him.

"We've got to hang together now," Sir Colin put in, pocketing the gun. "Otherwise, we haven't a hope. We must not squabble, laddie."

Mike shrugged, his good-looking cat-features darkened with his scowl. "I won't turn my back on you again, Drake," he said evenly. "We'll settle it later. But we'll settle it."

Alan said, "Suit yourself."

It was very cold now. But even the wind felt lifeless as night deepened over the earth. When the stars came, they were unrecognizable. The Milky Way alone looked familiar. Alan thought fantastically that its light might have left it at the very moment they had left their own world forever—to meet them here in an unimaginable rendezvous where the last dregs of time were ebbing from the world.

Moonrise roused them a little. The great pale disc came up slowly, tremendously, overpowering and desolately beautiful in the night of the world.

"Look," murmured Karen in a hushed voice. "You can see the craters and the dead seas—"

"Not close enough yet to cause quakes, I think," Sir Colin said, squinting at it. "Might be tremendous tidal waves, though, if any water's left. I wonder—"

He stopped quite suddenly, halting the others. A rift in the ground mists had drawn cloudy curtains aside, and there before them, in monstrous silhouette against the moon, stood the great black outlines of that shape they had glimpsed for a fleeting instant from the ship. Misshapen, asymmetrical, but too regular to be any natural formation.

Karen's voice was as thin as a voice in a dream. "Nothing that men ever made. . . ."

"It must be enormous," Sir Colin murmured. "Far away, but big—big! Well, we head for it, I suppose?"

"Of course we do." Karen spoke sharply. Command was in her voice for the first time since their awakening, as if she had only now fully aroused from a dream. Alan looked at her in surprise in the gray of the moonlight. Seeing a chance of survival, she had come alive. Life and color had flowed back into her.

"Come on," commanded the crisp, new voice. "Maybe there's a chance for us here after all. Sir Colin, let Mike have his gun again. We may need it."

"Don't expect too much, lassie," warned the Scotsman mildly, producing the revolver. "Most likely the place has been empty a thousand years."

"We've been acting like a pack of children," Karen declared sharply, swinging a keen stare about through the mist. "There're bird-things here—there may be others. Mike, you do a vanguard, will you? About twenty paces ahead unless the mist gets worse. Alan, drop back just a little and keep an eye out behind us. Sir Colin, you and I'll see that nothing sneaks up on us from the sides. We'll keep as close together as we can, but if we blunder into anything ahead, we mustn't all be caught at once."

Alan's ears burned a little as he obediently dropped back a few paces. When Karen awoke, she awoke with a vengeance. He should have thought of possible danger around them before now. They had all been walking in a dream—a dream of desolation and death, where nothing but themselves still breathed. But the birdmen lived, and there had been that great strange roaring that had shaken the earth.

As the moon rose higher, it seemed to draw mists from the ground. Presently the four drew closer together, so as not to lose each other. The pale, thick fogs were seldom more than waist high, but often they piled up into grotesque, twisted pillars and mounds, moving sluggishly as if half alive. Against the monstrous circle of the moon the citadel held steady, huge and enigmatic.

Out of the moving mists before them came something white as fog, coiling as the fog coiled. Something slow and pale—and dreadful. Mike Smith snatched out his gun. Karen made a futile gesture to stop him, but there was no need. It was all too evident that guns would be useless against this behemoth of a dying world.

Farther and farther, bigger and bigger, the great pale worm came sliding out of the mist. Alan's mouth went dry with sickened loathing as the thing coiled past, moving with a slow, unreal, sliding motion that was infinitely repellent. The creature was thick as a man's height; its body trailed off and vanished in the fog-veils. It was featureless, Alan thought. He could not see it clearly, and was grateful for that.

It neither sensed nor saw the humans. Monstrously it writhed past and was gone, slowly, silently, like a dream.

Sir Colin's voice was shaken as he spoke. "It's probably harmless. An adaptation—"

"God!" Mike licked his lips, staring after the vanished, misty thing. "God, what was it?"

Alan managed a grin. "A worm, Mike. Just a worm. Remember 'em?"

"Yeah." The other's voice was toneless. "But I wonder if everything is that big here."

The black citadel grew larger as they plodded on. They could see now that the unknown creators of that monstrous pile had dealt with mountainous masses of stone as though basalt had been clay. It was not basalt, of course; probably it was some artificial rock. Yet ordinary gravitational and architectural limitations seemed to have had no meaning to the Builders.

Half aloud, Alan mused, "Wonder how long we've been walking? My watch has stopped—quite a while ago, I suppose."

Sir Colin flashed him a whimsically sardonic glance.

"It'll need oiling, at least, before it runs again," he called back.

Alan smiled in turn.

"If we've slept for a million years—we've been remarkably well preserved. I mean our clothes and our ammunition. Powder doesn't last long, as a rule. Plenty of cartridges stored in nineteen nineteen were duds by nineteen forty."

(Sudden nostalgia, even for wars. . . . What tremendous battles had raged and ebbed over the ground they walked on now, before armies and ravaged lands together fell into dust?)

Sir Colin burred a laugh. "It wasna sleep, laddie. I think it was far more than suspended animation. Everything stopped. Did ye ever heard of stasis?"

Alan nodded. "The absolute zero? Slowing down the electronic orbits to stop the liberation of quanta."

"You know the catch-words," Sir Colin chuckled. "Now look: we grow old because we lose more energy than we can take in. Take, for example, a pool of water. A stream flows into it, and out of it. As the human organism acquires and loses energy. Now, come winter, what happens? There's a freeze, until the spring thaw."

"Spring!" Alan's laugh was harsh. He glanced around at the dark, desolate autumn of the world, an autumn hesitating on the verge of eternal winter that would freeze the universe forever. Sir Colin had dropped back until he walked abreast with Alan.

"Aye," he said. "The lochs are frozen with more than cold. The world's old, laddie. What lives in it now is the spawn of age—twisted abortions of evil. Mindless manbirds, worms gone mad with growth, what else we may never know." He shrugged wearily. "Yet you see my point. While the world died, we didna merely sleep. Something—perhaps a ray, or some sort of gas—halted our natural processes. The atomic structure of our bodies, our clothing, the powder in our cartridges—they must not have been subject to normal wear. The pool was frozen. My beard is no longer than it was when I last combed it."

Automatically, Alan fingered his own chin, where the stubble felt less than a few hours old. "And now we pick up where we left off," he said. "I ought to be hungry. But I'm not, yet."

"The ice breaks up slowly. Presently you'll be hungry enough. So will we all. And I've seen no food, except those flying things."

"They must eat. If we could follow them to water, there might be vegetation."

Sir Colin shook his head. "There'd not be much water left by now. And its saline content would be greater than Salt Lake—enough to poison fish, unless they were adapted to living in it. The same for vegetation."

"But the flying things—"

"Maybe, maybe. But what d'ye think they eat? Perhaps stuff we couldn't touch."

"Maybe we'll know, when we arrive." Alan nodded toward the monstrous citadel outlined against the moon.

"Whoever built that damned thing," the scientist said, with a curious note of horror in his voice, "I doubt strongly if their digestive systems were at all akin to ours. Have you noticed how wrong that geometry is, laddie? Based on nothing earthly. See?"

Alan squinted through the mists. The great fortress had grown almost mountain-huge, now. Moonlight did not reflect from the vast dark surfaces at all, so that the thing remained almost in silhouette, but they could see that it was composed of geometric forms which were yet strangely alien, polyhedrons, pyramids, pentagons, globes, all flung together as if without intelligent design. And yet each decoration was braced as though against tremendous stresses, or against a greater gravitational pull. Only high intelligence could have reared that vast structure towering above the mists of the plain, but it grew clearer at every step that the intelligence had not been human.

"The size of it—" Alan murmured, awe in his voice. Long before they reached the building they had been forced to strain their heads back to see the higher pinnacles. Now, as they neared the base of the walls, the sheer heights above them were vertiginous when they looked up.

Sir Colin put out a wondering hand toward the dead blackness of the wall.

"Eroded," he murmured. "Eroded—and God knows there must be little rainfall here. How old must it be?"

Alan touched the wall. It was smooth, cold, hard, seemingly neither stone nor metal.

"Notice how little light it reflects," Sir Colin said.

"Very low refractive index—seems to absorb the moonlight."

Yes, the black wall drank in the moonlight. The pale rays seemed to flow into that cliff like a shining river into a cavern. As Alan stared, it seemed to him that he was looking into a tunnel—a black, hollow emptiness that stretched illimitably before him, starless as interstellar gulfs.

He knew an instant of the same vertigo he had felt when he stepped out of the dead darkness of the room in the ship. And—yes, these darknesses were related. Each of them a negation, canceling out light and sound. This wall was something more than mere structural substance. It might not even be matter at all, as we know it, but something from outside, where the laws of earthly physics are suspended or impossibly altered.

Mike's hand was on his gun-butt. "I don't like this," he said, lips drawn back against his teeth.

"No more do I," Sir Colin said quietly. He was rubbing his bearded chin and looking up and down along the blank base of the wall. "I doubt if there's a way in—for us."

"There is no way," Alan heard his own voice saying with a timbre he did not recognize as his. "There is no door for us. The entrance is—there?" He tilted his head back and stared up at those tumbled pinnacles above.

From far away he heard Sir Colin's sharp, "Eh? Why d'ye say that, laddie?"

He looked down and into three pairs of keen, narrowed eyes that stared at him without expression. A sudden shock of distrust for all three of his companions all but rocked him back on his heels in that sudden, wordless moment. *What did they remember?*

For himself, he could not be sure now just what flash of memory had brought those strange words to his mind. He forced his voice to a normal tone, and said through stiff lips, "I don't know. Thinking of the flying things, I suppose. There certainly aren't any doors here."

Alan wondered if a deep tide of awareness was running among the three of them, shutting him out.

As for entering the building—he understood Mike Smith's feelings poignantly. If even Mike could feel it, then there must be something more than imagination to the strange, sick horror that rose like a dark tide in his mind whenever he thought of entering. Why should he behave like a hysterical child, afraid of the unknown? Perhaps because it was not entirely unknown to him. He shut his eyes, trying to think. Did he know what lay within the black citadel?

No. No pictures came. Only the dim thought of the Alien, and a very certain sense that the colossal building housed something unspeakable.

Mike Smith's urgent whisper broke into his bewildering memories.

"Someone's coming."

He opened his eyes. Waist-deep, the white mists swirled about them. In the distance, floating slowly toward the black citadel, a quasi-human figure moved through the fog.

"One of those bird-things?" Mike breathed, straining eagerly toward the distant shape. "I'll get it—"

"Mike!" Karen cautioned.

"I won't shoot it. I'll just see it doesn't get off the ground." He crouched into the mists, and slid away like a smoothly stalking cat, vanishing into the grayness.

Alan strained his eyes after the moving figure. It was not, he thought, a bird-creature. His heart was pounding with the excitement of finding something other than themselves moving in human shape through this dust of all humanity. The distant figure flowed curiously in all its outlines—as if, perhaps, it were not wholly human.

A big dark figure rose suddenly beside it. Mike, with outstretched arms. The gossamer shape sprang away from him with a thin, clear cry like a chord struck from vibrating strings. All its filmy outlines streamed away as it whirled toward the citadel and the watching humans.

A wind made the mists swirl confusingly. They heard Mike yell, and through the rolling dimness saw his dark shape and the pale, mist-colored shape dodging and running through the fog. It was like watching a shadow-play. Mike was not overtaking his quarry, but they could see that he was driving it closer and closer to them.

Alan leaned forward, avid excitement flaming through him. Here was an answer, he told himself eagerly—a tangible, living answer to all the riddles they could not solve. What manner of being dwelt here in this last death of the world?

Suddenly out of the depths of a mist-wave that had rolled blindingly over them he heard a soft thudding and in the gray blindness something rushed headlong against him.

Automatically his arms closed about it.

II

CARCASILLA

His first impression was one of incredible fragility. In the instant while mist still blinded him, he knew that he held a girl, but a girl so inhumanly fragile that he thought her frantic struggles to escape might shatter the delicate bones by their very frenzy.

Then the fog rolled back again, and moonlight poured down upon them. Mike came panting up out of the mist, calling, "Did you catch it?" Karen and Sir Colin pushed forward eagerly, staring. Alan did not speak a word. He was looking down, speechless, at what he held in his arms.

The captive's struggles had ceased when light came back around them. She hung motionless in Alan's embrace, head thrown back, staring up at him. Not terror, but complete bewilderment, made her features a mask of surprise.

They were unbelievably delicate features. The very

skull beneath must not be common bone, but some exquisite structure carved of ivory. Her face had the flawless, unearthly perfection of a flower. That was it—she had a flower's delicacy, overbred, painstakingly cultured and refined out of all kinship with the coarse human prototype. Even her hair seemed so fine that it floated upon the misty air, only settling now about her shoulders as her struggles ceased. The gossamer robe that had made her outlines waver so strangely in the fog fell in cobwebby folds which every breath fluttered.

Looking down at her, Alan was more awestruck than he might have been had she been the wholly outré thing he expected. This delicate, hothouse creature could have no conceivable relation with the dead desert around them.

She was staring up at him with that odd astonishment in great dark eyes fringed with silver lashes. And as the deep gaze locked with his, he remembered for a swimming moment the instant of mental probing in the Tunisian desert, before the world blanked out forever. But he knew that it had been the Alien who probed their minds outside the ship. And the Alien could have no possible connection with this exquisitely fragile thing.

Sir Colin's rasping voice was saying, "She's human! Would ye believe it? She's human! That means we're not alone in this dead world!"

"Don't let her go," Karen cried excitedly. "Maybe she'll lead us to food!"

Alan scarcely heard them. He was watching the girl's face as she lifted her eyes to the heights of blackness above them. Alan's gaze swept up to the fantastic turrets. Nothing—nothing at all. But the girl stared as if she could see something up there invisible to them. Perhaps she could. Perhaps her senses were keener than theirs.

And then suddenly, terrifyingly, Alan knew what it was she could see. There was a mysterious kinship indeed between her and the Alien. He could see nothing, but he felt invisible pressure about them all. A presence, intangible as the wind, filling the moonlit dark as it had filled the Tunisian valley by the ship. Something that watched from the great black heights—watched, but with no human eyes.

Karen said, "She's not afraid any more. Notice that?"

Alan looked down. The girl was not searching the haunted heights of the citadel any more; she was searching Alan's face instead, and all the terror had vanished from those exquisitely frail features. It was as if that alien being of the dark had breathed a word to her, and all terror had vanished. Something, somehow, connected her with this monstrous citadel and the Alien.

"Ye feel it, too, eh?" Sir Colin's voice was a burring hush, his accent strong.

"Feel what?"

"Danger, laddie. Danger. This isn't our own time. Human motives are certain to have altered—perhaps a great deal. The two and two of the human equation don't equal four any more. And—" He hesitated. "We no longer have any gauge to know what's human and what is not."

Mike Smith was staring coldly at the girl. "She's human enough to eat food, anyway. It's our job to find out what and where she gets it."

It was curious, thought Alan, that the girl who so

certainly shared an indefinable affinity with the Alien did not make them shudder, too.

Now, she laid two hands like exquisite carvings in ivory upon Alan's chest, and gently pushed herself free. He let her go half doubtfully, but she did not move more than a pace or two away, then stood waiting, a luminous query in her eyes.

On an impulse Alan tapped his chest and pronounced his own name clearly, in the immemorial pantomime of the stranger laying a foundation for common speech. The girl's face lighted up as if a lamp had been lit to glow through the delicate flesh. Alan was to learn very well that extravagant glow of interest when something touched a responding facet of her mind.

"A-lahn?" She imitated the gesture. "Evaya," she said, her voice like a tinkling silver bell.

Mike Smith said impatiently. "Tell her we're hungry." The girl glanced at him uneasily, and when Sir Colin muttered agreement she stepped back a pace, her gossamer robe wavering up about her. Alan was the only man there she did not seem to fear a little.

With surprising lack of success, he tried to show her by gestures that they wanted food. Later, he would learn why food and drink meant so little to this strange dweller in a dying world. Now, he was merely puzzled. Finally, at random, he pointed away across the plain. She must have come from somewhere . . . There was no response on Evaya's face. He tried again, until a glow of understanding lighted suddenly behind her delicate features, and she nodded, the pale hair lifting to her motion.

"*Carcasilla*," she said, in that thin, trilling voice.

"Which means exactly nothing," Karen remarked.

Evaya gave her a glance of dislike. She had been almost pointedly ignoring the warm, bronze beauty of the other girl.

Sir Colin shook his head.

"Maybe the place she came from."

"Not the citadel?"

"I think not. She was going toward it when we saw her, remember."

"Why?"

The Scotsman rubbed his beard. "I don't know that, of course. I don't like it. Superficially, this girl seems harmless enough. But I have a strong feeling the citadel is not. And she seems to—to share a sort of affinity with it. See?"

Evaya's eyes had followed the lifted gaze of the others, but she seemed to feel none of their aversion to the monstrous structure. Her eyes held awe—perhaps worship. But Alan sensed, for a brief, shuddering second, a feeling of unseen eyes watching coldly.

Perhaps Karen sensed it, too. "Come on," she said. "Let's get out of here."

With careful sign-language, Alan tried to tell Evaya what they wanted. She still hesitated, looking up at the unresponding heights. But presently she turned away and beckoned to Alan, setting off in the direction from which she had come. By her look she did not greatly care if the others followed or not.

"Fair enough," Sir Colin muttered, swinging into step beside Alan.

They plodded on again in the pale moonlight of this empty world, through monotonous waist-high mists. The dead lands around them slid by unchanging. Once they heard, far away, the faint thunder they had noticed before, and the ground trembled slightly underfoot. Evaya ignored it.

Alan was growing tired. A faint throbbing in one arm had begun to annoy him, and glancing down, he realized with an almost vertiginous sense of time-lapse that the graze of a Nazi bullet still traced its unhealed furrow across his forearm. Nazis and bullets were dust on the face of the forgetful planet, but in the stasis of the ship even that wound had remained fresh, unchanging.

Sir Colin's deep voice interrupted the thought. "This girl," the Scotchman said. "She's no savage, Drake. You've noticed that? Obviously she's the product of some highly developed culture. Almost a forced culture. Unnaturally perfect."

"Unnaturally?"

"She's too fragile. It's abnormal. I think her environment must be completely shielded from any sort of danger. It may be—"

"*Carcasilla!*" cried Evaya's ringing silver voice. "*Carcasilla!*" And she pointed ahead.

Alan saw that what he had taken for some time past to be the reflection of moonlight on a polished rock was no reflection at all. A glowing disc, twenty feet high, slanted along the slope of a low hillock a little way ahead.

A disc? It *was* moonlight, or the moon itself, tropic-large, glowing with a lambent yellow radiance in the dust, like an immense flat jewel.

Evaya walked lightly to the softly shining moon, stood silhouetted against it, waiting for the rest to follow her. And as she stood there in bold outline, the mist of her garments only a shadow around her, Alan realized suddenly that fragile though she might be, Evaya was no child. He knew a moment of curious jealousy as the smooth long limbs of an Artemis stood black against the moon-disc before them all, round and delicate with more than human perfection. All her lines were the lovely ones of the huntress goddess, and the moon behind her should have been crescent, not full.

Evaya stepped straight into the shining moon and vanished.

"A door!" Alan's voice was strained.

"Do you think we'd better follow?" Karen asked in an undertone. "I don't quite trust that girl."

Mike laughed, his strong white teeth showing. "I'm hungry and thirsty. Also—" He slapped his holster, and stepped forward confidently, pressing against the shining portal. And—it did not yield.

He turned back a face of frowning bewilderment. "It's solid, Sir Colin—"

Alan and the Scotsman followed Karen to the threshold. The barrier seemed intangible, yet their hands slid along the disc of light as though it were glass. Alan thought briefly that the thing was like the substance of the citadel—materialized light, as that had been solid darkness. Had the same hands created them both?

"The girl went through it easily enough." Sir Colin was gnawing his lip, scowling. "Curious. It may be a barrier to keep out enemies—but why did she lead us here, if she meant to lock us out?"

"Maybe she didn't know we couldn't follow," Alan said, and—before anyone could answer, Evaya stepped back through the barrier. Her eyes searched them, puzzled. She beckoned. Alan pointed to the shining wall; then, despairing of explanations, pressed himself futilely against the strange barricade. Understanding lighted magically, as always, behind Evaya's ivory face. She nodded at them confidently, and slipped like a shadow into the moon-disc.

"It's no barrier to her, obviously," Sir Colin grunted. "Remember what I said—that she may not be quite human, as we know the word?"

"She's human enough to understand what's wrong," Alan snapped, curiously on the defensive for Evaya's sake. "She won't—"

He paused, startled. A sound had come out of the darkness behind them. A sound? No. . . . A call in the brain, echoing from the desert they had crossed. All of them heard it; all of them turned to stare back the way they had come. It was utterly silent there, the starlight shining on low mists, dimmer now that the moon was gone. Nothing moved.

And yet there was—something—out there. Something that summoned.

Alan knew the feeling. It was coming—coming across the plain on their tracks, coming like a dark cloud he could sense without seeing. The Presence of the Tunisian valley, of the space ship, of the citadel. Each time nearer, stronger . . . this time—demanding. He could sense it sweeping forward over the dust of their tracks like some monstrous, shapeless beast snuffing at their footsteps, nearing, nearing. . . .

And it summoned. Something deep within Alan drew him out, away from the others. But revulsion held him motionless. His brain seemed to move inside his skull at

EARTH'S LAST CITADEL

the urge of that unseen Presence coming through the darkness. The cold starlight revealed nothing. He heard Sir Colin breathing hard, heard Mike curse. A figure moved past him—Karen. He caught her arm.

"No! Don't—"

She turned a white, drained face toward him.

Rainbow light sprang out from behind them. It glowed cloudily across the plain, their shadows standing long and dark across it. But it showed nothing more.

"The door—she's opened it," Mike said in a harsh, choked voice. "Come on, for God's sake!"

Alan turned, pulling Karen with him. It was like turning one's back on darkness where devils lurked. His spine crawled with the certainty of something deadly coming swiftly nearer. The great moon-disc was no longer flat now, as he faced it, but the open end of a long and glowing corridor of light. Sir Colin lurched through after Mike; then Alan and Karen stumbled in. Alan looked back just as the golden veil of the doorway swept down to blot out the desert. In that instant he thought he saw something vague and shadowy moving forward through the mist. Like a stalking beast along their tracks in the dust. Something dark in the moving fog-wreaths. . . .

Alan put out his hand to touch the golden veil, and found the same glass-smooth barrier that had barred them from entering, stretched now across the doorway they had just passed.

Karen said shakily, "Do you think it can get in?"

Sir Colin, his voice unsteady, but his scientist's brain keen in spite of it, said in the thick Scots of emotional strain, "I—I dinna think so, lassie. Else it wouldna ha' tried so hard to—to capture us before we passed the barrier."

Mike Smith's laugh was harsh. "*Capture* us? What gives you that idea?"

Alan said nothing. His eyes were impassive slits under the full lids, his mouth tight. There was no use in pretending any more about one thing—the Presence was no figment of remembered dreams. It was real enough to be deadly, and it had followed them, with what unimaginable purpose he could only guess. But not, he thought —capture. Mike's primitive instinct was right. Mike knew death when it came snuffing at his heels.

"*A-lahn?*" It was Evaya's voice, beyond them. Alan looked over Mike's shoulder and saw the girl's exquisite gossamer-veiled figure in the full light of the strange golden corridor. But she was not looking at them now. Her eyes were on the closed barrier through which they had come, and her face was the face of one listening. For one quite horrible moment Alan guessed that the dark thing which had swept along their tracks in the desert was calling her through the barrier of solid light. Undoubtedly there had been some evanescent communion between her and the Presence at the citadel; was it speaking again here?

She was lovelier than ever, here in the full golden light, more flawlessly perfect, with the exquisite, inhuman perfection of a flower or a figurine. She had a flower's coloring, rose and ivory white, with deep violet eyes. Here in the light her hair was a pale shade between gold and silver, and with a curious sort of iridescence when she turned her head.

She was turning it now, as if some faint call had reached her through the closed door. But it must have been very faint, because she shrugged a little and smiled up at Alan, pointing along the corridor ahead.

"*Carcasilla,*" she said, with pride in her voice. "*Carcasilla—vyenne!*"

The great golden passage swept up before them in a glowing arc whose farther end they could not see. Evaya gestured again and started up that glowing, iridescent incline.

As they advanced along the curved floor of the tunnel, Alan realized that this corridor had never been designed for human feet to travel. It was a tube, its curved floor smooth and unworn by passing feet. And its upward slant grew steeper. Human builders would have put steps here, or a ramp. Now they were clinging to the floor and walls with flattened palms, slipping between paces.

Even for Evaya, progress was difficult. She smiled back now and then when her own sure feet slipped a little on the steeply climbing, hollowed floor.

Alan had been keeping a wary lookout behind them as they slipped and stumbled along the tube. But no darkness was following, no voiceless summons echoed in his brain. The Presence, the Alien—whatever it had been—must temporarily at least have been stopped by the moon-disc of solid light which had dropped behind them.

After what seemed to Alan a long time, the tube abruptly leveled, and Evaya stepped aside, smiling. "Carcasilla!" she said proudly.

They stepped out of the tube upon a platform that jutted from the face of the cliff. At their feet, a ramp ran steeply down; to left and right the platform circled out around the rock walls in a spiderweb gallery, as far as Alan could see. It was a curious gallery with a tilted rail around it. Automatically the four from the world's youth moved forward to lean upon the rail and look.

Before them lay the blue-lit vista of a vast cavern. And in the cavern—a city.

Such a city as mankind had never visualized even in dreams. It was like—yes, like Evaya herself, delicate and fragile as some artifice, with a beauty heartbreaking in its sheer perfection. It was not a city as mankind understands them. It was a garden in stone and crystal; it was a dream in three dimensions—it was anything but a city built by man.

And it was—silent.

The whole cavern was one vast violet dream where no gravity prevailed, no rain ever fell, no sun shone, no winds blew. Someone's dream had crystallized into glass and marble bubbles and great loops of avenues hanging upon empty air to fill the blue hollow of the cavern. But it had been no human dream.

Following the others down the ramp reluctantly, Alan saw a further confirmation of that suspicion. For the balcony rail was pitched at a strange angle, and set at an awkward height from the floor, yet obviously it was meant to lean upon. The gallery, like the tube that led to it, had not been designed for any human creature. Something else had dreamed the dream of Carcasilla; something else had planned and built it; something else had set this gallery around the cavern so that it might lean its unimaginable body against it and brood over the beauty of its handiwork.

They stood at the edge of a swimming abyss. Here, there were no floating islands of buildings overhead, no roofs below. Only the mirrored pavement. But springing out from the foot of the ramp, there climbed a long, easy spiral of ascending steps, down which pale water seemed to flow, breaking in a series of scalloping ripples at their feet, and fading into the blue-green pavement they had been walking. Obviously it could not be water, but the illusion was so perfect they drew back from the lapping ripples instinctively.

All Carcasilla defied gravity, but this was the most outrageous defiance they had yet seen. The broad, graceful curve of the waterfalling steps swept out and around over sheer space, unsupported, made four diminishing turns and ended at the base of a floating tower which apparently had no other support than the coil of flying steps.

And the tower was a tower of water. Its vague, slim, gothic outlines were veiled in pale torrents that fell as straight as rain down over the hidden walls and went gushing away along the steps. The place looked aloof and withdrawn from the rest of the brightly blooming buildings.

Evaya set her foot upon the first step, and smiled back across her shoulder, nodding toward the raining tower above. "*Flande*," she said.

Dubiously, they followed her up the spiral, at first watching their feet incredulously as they found themselves walking dryshod upon the waterfall whose torrent slid away untouched beneath their soles. But when they had mounted a few steps, they found it unwise to look down. Their heads spun as they walked upon sliding water over an abyss.

The tower of rain should have roared with its falling torrents. But there was no sound as the illusory water swept downward before them, near enough to touch. And no door opened anywhere.

While the four newcomers stood gaping up, for the moment too engrossed to speak, Evaya stepped forward confidently and laid her exquisite small hands flat against the rain. They should have vanished to the delicate wrists, with water foaming around them. But the illusion evidently dwelt beneath the surface of the tower, for the rain slipped away unhindered beneath her palms.

Unhindered? After a moment the torrents began to sway apart, like curtains withdrawing. A slit was widening and widening in the wall.

"Flande . . ." Evaya said, a little breathlessly.

The opening, wide now, stopped expanding. Within it were rainbow mists like sunlight caught in the spray of a waterfall. They began to dissipate, and faintly through them Alan glimpsed a face, gigantic as a god's. But it was no godly face. It was very human. And it was asleep. . . .

Youth was here upon these quiet features, but not a youth like Evaya's, warm and confident and glowing with inner radiance. This was a timeless youth, graven as if in marble, and as meaningless as youth upon the face of a statue a thousand years old.

As they stood silent, the closed lids rose slowly. And very old, very wise eyes looked into Alan's, coldly, as if through the clouded memories of a thousand years. The lips moved, just a trifle.

"*Evaya—*" said a deep, resonant, passionless voice. "*Evaya—va esten da s'ero.*"

The girl beside them hesitated. "*Mai ra–*" she began.

The voice of Flande did not rise, but a deeper and more

commanding thunder seemed to beat distantly in its tones. Evaya glanced uncertainly at the little group behind her, singling out Alan with her eyes. He grinned at her tightly. She gave him an uncertain smile. Then she turned away from the great face above them and moved slowly toward the descending ramp.

Mike Smith said sharply, "Is she running out on us? I'll—"

Abruptly, he fell silent, lips drawn back, blunt features hardening into amazed wariness, as a voice spoke soundlessly within the minds of all of them.

Very softly it came at first, then gaining in assurance as though questing fingers had found contact. Wordless, inarticulate, yet clear as any spoken tongue, the voice said:

"I have sent Evaya away. She will wait at the tower's foot, while I question you."

Alan risked a sidewise look at Sir Colin. The Scotchman was leaning forward, his head cocked grotesquely, his beak nose reminding Alan of a parrot investigating some new morsel. There was no fear in Sir Colin's face, only profound interest. Karen showed no expression whatever, though her bright green eyes were narrowed. As for Mike Smith, he stood alertly, with a coiled-spring poise, waiting.

"Do you understand me?" the voice murmured soundlessly.

"We understand." Sir Colin spoke for them all, after a quick glance around. "This is telepathy, I think?"

"My mind touches yours. So we speak in the tongue that knows no race or barrier. Yes, it is telepathy. But speak aloud; it is easier for me to sift your minds."

Alan touched Sir Colin's arm, giving him a brief look of warning.

"Wait a minute," he said. "We've a few questions to ask ourselves."

Flande's great veiled eyes flashed—a streak of silver fire leaped out above their heads with a crackle of dangerous sharpness.

All of the little group cowered away under it as the sword-blade of silver light flashed across the platform where they stood.

The shelf was wide here, and of translucent clarity, as if they stood on a depthless pool of clear water. There was only quiet emptiness below them as they stumbled backward, the fiery menace of Flande's glance burning tangibly past their heads.

Then Flande laughed, cool and distant. And the burning silver sword broke suddenly into a rain of silver droplets that sparkled like stars. Sparkled and came showering down around them. Karen flung up an arm to shield her eyes; Mike swore in German. The other two stood tense and rigid, waiting for the stars to engulf them all.

But Flande laughed again, a thousand years away behind his veil of memories, and the shower fell harmlessly past them and sank glittering into the pellucid depths of the shelf on which they stood. Down and down. . . . And the twinkling points began to dance with colors.

Alan watched them in a curious, timeless trance. . . . And then—under his feet the glassy paving crumbled like rotten ice. He was falling— He threw himself flat, and the support held him briefly—briefly. . . . Then, in a crackle of broken glass, he plunged downward.

Flande's cool laughter sounded a third time.

"Stand up," he said. "There is no danger. See—my magic is withdrawn."

Miraculously, it was so. The platform spread unbroken beneath's Alan's hands, a surface of quiet water. Crimson-faced, he scrambled up, hearing the scuff of feet about him as the others scrambled, too. Karen's lips were white. Sir Colin's twisted into a wry half-grin. Mike muttered in German again, and Alan had a sudden irrelevant thought that Flande had made an enemy just now—for what that enmity was worth. The rest of them could accept this magic for what it was—telepathy, perhaps, group hypnotism—but to Mike it was personal humiliation and would demand a personal revenge . . .

For a moment, they stood hesitant, facing the great visage that looked down aloofly from the tower, no one quite knowing what move to make. Flande spoke.

"Fools question me," he said. "I think you will not question me again. These you have seen are the least of my powers. And you are not welcome here, for you have troubled my dreams."

The brooding gaze swept out past them all, plumbing distances far beyond the cavern walls that hemmed in Carcasilla.

"You are strange people, from what I see in your minds. But perhaps not strange enough to interest me for long."

Alan said, "What do you want of us, then?"

"You will answer my questions. You will tell me who you are, and whence you come, and why."

"All right. There's no secret about us. But after that, what?"

"Come here," Flande said.

Alan took a cautious step forward, his nerves wirestrung. The vast face watched him impassively.

Still cautiously, Alan advanced, step by careful step, straight toward that enigmatic doorway. No sound from the others warned him. Only the airman's trained instinct, almost a sixth sense, told Alan his equilibrium was going. The pavement seemed as solid as ever under his advancing foot. But sheer instinct made him twist in the middle of a stride and hurl himself backward, scrambling on the edge of an abyss he could sense but not see. The surprised faces of the others stared at him.

He reached out gingerly, exploring the platform until his fingers curled over the edge. Below lay the swimming violet depths of Carcasilla. One more step in the blindness of his hypnotic trance would have plunged him down.

"What the devil, lad—" Sir Colin rasped.

Alan got up. "I almost walked over the edge," he said.

Sir Colin said gently. "His hypnotic powers are very strong. We *thought* you were walking straight toward him."

"And that the platform was bigger than it really is," Alan finished, his mouth grim. He swung toward the tower. "Okay. I get the idea. You're going to kill us?"

Flande smiled gravely. "I do not yet know."

The great visage looked down at them and beyond them, fathomless weariness in its eyes. And Alan, returning that distant stare, wondering at his own daring in provoking the caprice of this incredible being of the world's end. That enormous face looked human. . . . A three-dimensional projection upon some giant screen, or only illusion, like the other things that had happened? Or was Flande really human at all?

Perhaps the face was a mask, hiding something unimaginable. . . .

"Look here," Alan said, making his voice confident. "If you can read minds, why question us? I think—"

Flande's eyes, brooding on something far beyond them, suddenly narrowed with a look of very human satisfaction. "You will think no more!" said the voiceless speech in their minds. It swelled with a sort of scornful triumph. "Did you think I cared where you came from, little man? I know where you are going. . . ."

From somewhere behind them, and below, a hoarse shout rang out upon the violet silence of Carcasilla. Close after it, Evaya's scream lifted, pure silver, like a struck chord. Flande's voice halted the confusion among the four beneath him as Alan took a long stride toward the stair, and Sir Colin whirled, and Mike reached smoothly for his gun.

"Wait," said Flande. "There is no escape for you now. I do not want you in Carcasilla. You are barbarians. We have no room for you here. So I have summoned other barbarians, from the wild ways outside our city, to save me the trouble of killing you. Do you wonder why I practiced those tricks of illusion a little while ago? It was to give the barbarians time to come here, through the gate I opened for them. . . . Look behind you!"

A shuddering vibration began to shake the stair; the hoarse cries from below came nearer, and the thud of mounting feet. Then Evaya came flying up into view, looking back in terror over her shoulder through the cloud of her floating hair.

"Terasi!" she cried. "The *Terasi!*" . . .

Flande met her wild appeal with a chilly glance, his eyes half-closed in passionless triumph. The godlike head shook twice. Then the slitted door began to close. Mike Smith yelled something in German, and lifted his gun. But, before he could take aim, the valve had closed and vanished; curtains of rain gushed unbroken down the wall. Flande was gone.

Thumping steps mounted the last spiral. A group of ragged savages came rushing up toward them, their faces—curiously clouded with fear—taking on grimness and purpose as they saw their quarry. The leader yelled again, brandishing the clubbed branch of some underground tree.

Clearly these were raiders from some other source than Carcasilla. They looked incredibly out of place in this city of jeweled bubbles, with their heavy, muscular bodies scarred and hairy under the tatters of brown leather garments. All were fair and yellow haired. And on each face, beneath the wolfish triumph, was a certain look of fear and iron-hard desperation.

No—not all. One man was taller than the others, magnificently built, with the great muscles of an auroch, and a gargoyle face. His tangled fair hair was bound with a metal circlet; beneath it black eyes looked out without fear, but warily and grimly purposeful. A new wound slashed red across his tremendous chest, and the muscles rolled appallingly as he brandished his club. He had all of a gorilla's superhuman strength and ferocity, but controlled in a human body and far more dangerous because of it. Now he rushed on up the steps at the head of the raiders, yelling in a great bell-like voice.

This was no place for fighting hand to hand. The steps were too narrow over that dizzy blue gulf, and the water sliding down their spiral looked slippery if it was not.

But it was too late now to do anything but fight. Alan was nearest to the charging savages. And he had no time to think. The leader's deep bellow of triumph made the glass walls ring faintly about them as he came thundering up the steps, club lifted.

He came on straight for Alan, a towering, massive figure.

Blind instinct hurled Alan forward, his gun leaping to his hand. But something checked his finger on the trigger. He could not overcome a strong feeling that he must not fire in Carcasilla—that the walls would come shattering down around them from the concussion in this hushed city. He reversed the gun in his hand, and swung it, club-like, under the lifted weapon of the barbarian.

And that was a mistake. It was one of the few times that Alan Drake had ever underestimated an opponent. The club whistled down past Alan's shoulder, missing him as he dodged. But the giant dodged Alan's gun in turn, and his other hand moved with lightning speed. A flash of silver sang through the air.

White-hot pain darted through Alan's wrist. His hand went lax, and the gun clattered to the water-gushing steps. Alan looked down at the drops of blood splattering from his arm, where a shining metal dart with metal vanes to guide it transfixed his wrist. These were not quite the barbarians they looked, then, armed with things like that. . . .

Plucking the metal dart from the wound, Alan tensed to meet the charging man.

Hot fury blazed up in him. He hurled himself sidewise toward his fallen gun, catching it on the very verge of the steps. Behind him, Mike Smith roared with a savage exultation that echoed the gargoyle's shout, and cleared Alan's stooping body with one long, catlike step. The gunman's lips were flattened back from his teeth and his eyes glowed oddly yellow. Mike Smith was in his element. Elsewhere, he might be ill at ease; here he functioned with smooth precision.

But not quite smooth enough. For before his feet struck the steps beyond Alan, the scarred man had sprung to meet him, one sandaled foot lashing out in an unexpected kick at Mike's gun. Mike twisted sidewise instinctively—and then the gargoyle had him. Those mightily muscled arms closed crushingly about his ribs.

All this Alan saw as his fingers came down on the cool butt of his gun. Behind him, he had a glimpse of Karen and Sir Colin circling desperately, trying to get clear aim over Alan's head. But before they could do it, the man had lifted Mike Smith by the neck and crotch with one easy motion, the muscles crawling under his tattered leather, and hurled his captive straight in their faces. Almost in the same motion he sprang forward in a high leap and smashed down full upon Alan, whose finger was tightening on the trigger.

Alan had a momentary surge of sheer wonder at the lightning tactics of this savage even as he tried futilely to roll away beneath those crushing feet. Then the man's great weight crashed down and in a screaming blaze of pain oblivion blanked him out of the fight.

He was aware of shouts and trampling feet that receded into distance or into oblivion—he did not care.

After a while, he knew vaguely that the torrents of rain had parted again to let Flande's young-old face look down at him. Evaya's voice from somewhere near was demanding—demanding something. . . . He felt Flande's cold, pale stare, felt the enmity in it. He thought dimly that Evaya was asking something on his behalf and Flande denying it.

He heard Evaya's voice ring with sudden defiance. But before its echoes ceased to sound, he fell into a cloudy sleep that was almost as deep as death, drowning all other thoughts.

Uneven lightning-jabs of pain roused him presently, and he knew he was being carried with difficulty on the shoulders of—of whom?—Evaya's people? It didn't matter. Between sleeping and waking, he saw the bubble domes of Carcasilla sliding by.

And now they were moving down a far-flung curve of crystal stairs toward a vast basin of onyx and rose marble which stretched across the widest space he had yet seen in Carcasilla. Its edges were curved and carved into breakers of marble foam. Light brimmed the basin like water, violet, dimly translucent, rippling with constant motion.

They carried him out into the basin, toward a vast, towering, wavering column out of which seemed to pulse all the violet light that illuminated Carcasilla. It was a column of flame, a fountain of uprushing light. . . . Now he could feel the brimming pool lap up about him, cool, infinitely refreshing.

He could see the smooth floor underfoot, dimly beneath the blue-violet surface. He could see a pedestal of white marble, distorted by refraction, out of which the great flame sprang. It must, he thought vaguely, rush up from some source underground, straight through the marble as if it were not there. . . .

They carried him into that light—laid him on the marble pedestal—and he could breathe more easily here in the blue-violet flame than he had in the air outside—breathe against the white-hot pain of his ribs. . . .

The soft, rushing coolness all around him was washing the pain away. He was weightless, his body scarcely touching the marble. Even his hair strained at the roots, and currents swung him this way and that, gently, easily. The flame washed up through his very flesh, streaming coolly, sending bubbles of sensation through his body. Then violet sleep soothed all the pain out of his consciousness. He gave himself up to it, swaying with the uprush of light that possessed every atom of his body.

When he again became conscious of his surroundings, he lay upon cushions in a globe-shaped room through whose aquamarine walls seeped a light that was the very color of sleep itself.

Time passed vaguely as in a dream. The silvery-haired people of Carcasilla tiptoed in to whisper over him, and though he could not remember having seen them before, they were familiar to his unquestioning mind. Evaya sat beside him on the cushions oftenest of all. And later, she walked beside him on tours of Carcasilla when his steps were slow but no longer unsteady, and no memory of pain attended any motion.

He had no memories at all. The roaring, ruinous world he had left millenniums ago, the dead world where he had wakened, were alike forgotten in this strange dream-like state. He did not miss the companions who had vanished on the steps to Flande's house; he did not wonder where the barbarians had gone or whence they had come. Whatever was, was good.

Alan came to understand many of the words in the Carcasillians' liquid speech, that through sheer repetition grew familiar. And into his drugged mind knowledge crept slowly, as the soft voice of the fragile folk grew more understandable.

They told him of the fountain's magic. It gave immortality. All who bathed in its pulsing light were immortal, as long as they renewed the bathing at intervals. Even Flande came to the fountain at intervals—the voices said.

"Beware of Flande," they dinned into his dulled mind. *"His spells strike without warning. You must be strong —and awake! —to battle him, if battle must come."*

And other things the soft voices of Carcasilla whispered to Alan. He felt neither hunger nor thirst; the fountain breathed out all he needed to live. When the Carcasillians bathed in it, all ills were soothed, all wants healed. And when they wearied of life, the fountain gave them—sleep.

For they grew weary, here in their perfect, sterile world. When they had explored all of Carcasilla, and knew every bridge and building, and every face, and boredom began to trouble them—then they went below the fountain and took the Sleep. Memories were washed away—when they woke again, Carcasilla was new, and everyone in it, and life began afresh.

Thus it had been since the beginning. Lost in the Lethe of a thousand Great Sleeps were the origins of Carcasilla. Yet there were legends. The Light-Wearers had made it, and peopled it. The Light-Wearers had gone long since, but Carcasilla remained, a monument to their unearthly dreams. And the dwellers in Carcasilla were part of the dream that had reared the city.

Only Flande had never taken the Sleep. Only Flande —and the gods, perhaps—remembered all that had happened since the first days. He was afraid of forgetting something—his power, or a secret he held.

Awaken, A-lahn!

Strong the summons shrilled in his brain. For minutes or hours or days, he thought dimly, he had been hearing it. And now—suddenly enough—the curtain slipped away, and was gone from his half-sleeping mind.

It came without warning. He was sitting with Evaya in the mouth of the aquamarine globe, with a great sweep of the city spread out below them. One moment the fantastic vista beneath was a familiar, scarcely noticed thing—the next, a cloud seemed to withdraw, and colors and shapes and distances sprang into focus so sharp that for an instant it almost blinded him.

Alan leaped to his feet, and Evaya rose lightly beside him.

She smiled at him anxiously. And Alan, without an instant's hesitation or thought, leaned forward and took her into his arms. In a moment the spinning world and his spinning brain slowed and steadied, and nothing had any significance at all except the vibrant responding aliveness of the girl in his embrace.

Alan thought he had never known what it was to kiss a girl before. This strong, lithe body was not afraid of the full pressure his arms could bring to bear. She was not, after all, so fragile as she looked. It was like embracing a figure of tempered steel that answered the pressure with a singing resilience, quivering and alive with more than human aliveness.

Evaya stepped back.

"Now you *are* awake!" she said breathlessly, with a little dazzled smile. "But we have no time to talk of anything but Flande now. I called you so long, day after day. But you were not yet healed. The fountain still kept you in its sleep."

Alan caught his breath, remembrance coming back with an overwhelming rush.

"That was all real? Not delirium?"

"Real enough. Your sleep was deep—and Flande still stays his hand. I think—I am afraid—perhaps he waits only until you awake. . . ."

III

THE WAY OF THE GODS

FLANDE! Flande and the tower of rain, and the battle on the water-falling steps. It all came back to Alan in an avalanche of vivid memories. Questions crowded upon questions until his tongue tripped. He stammered over them for a moment, then said simply, "What happened?" and waited almost dizzily for the answer. Evaya smiled again.

But she sobered quickly.

"They took away your friends," she told him. "The Terasi, I mean. There was a great fight there on the steps. The evil young man fought terribly, but they took him at last. They struck the red girl on the head and carried her off senseless." Evaya looked a little pleased, in spite of herself. She had made no secret of her aversion toward Karen. "The old man went quite peacefully when he saw there was no hope. He seemed almost interested. I saw him trying to talk to the Terasi leader as they went down the steps."

Alan grinned. In the sudden strangeness of this alien city, it was good to hear one familiar thing about someone he knew. That would be Sir Colin—coolly examining the headsman's axe as it fell toward his own neck. He said quickly:

"Where did they go?"

Evaya shook her head, the silvery hair clouding out around her. "Nobody knows. The Terasi live somewhere outside Carcasilla, in the wilderness underground. Flande put a magic on them and brought them here. And afterward, when you were crushed by the barbarian's blow, he refused to let me bathe you in the fountain to heal your hurts."

Alan nodded, remembering dimly. "You—you changed his mind, didn't you?"

Evaya's face lighted. "I defied him. But—but shivering inside, for fear he might destroy me. I don't know how I found the courage to do it, unless—sometimes I have thought I was once the priestess who opened the doors of Carcasilla to the gods when the gods still lived. Long ago. But I am immortal, of course. Like you."

Alan looked at her silently. After a while he said, "I was wondering if I'd dreamed that."

She shook her head.

"No. It's quite true. All who bathe in the fountain live forever, so long as they renew the baths. You did not dream it. The gods made us so."

"The gods?"

She pointed. Far off through the city Alan could see a disc of blackness set against the cavern wall, tiny in the distance. Before it stood something so bright that its outlines blurred before his eyes.

"The statue of the Light-Wearer," Evaya said, reverence in her voice. "They made Carcasilla and us, for their pleasure. They lighted the fountain, that we might live eternally. Very long ago, I think I was their priestess, as I say—I opened the doors when they called. For there were good Light-Wearers and some—not good. Some who might have destroyed us. So the two doors into Carcasilla can be opened only from within, at the summons of the gods. But the gods, of course, are dead. . . ."

Evaya lifted a troubled gaze to his. "Has one of the gods come back?" she asked him.

Alan shook his head. "You tell *me*," he said.

Evaya said presently, "I felt the call from far away, very weak. And I remembered from many sleeps ago. . . . All memories are washed away in the fountain when we take the great sleep, but somehow, I knew the call. So I went up to the citadel where the gods once lived—and you were there, A-lahn. But I think—A-lahn, I think this god is not one of the good Light-Wearers. If it is a god. I am not sure. . . . I don't wish to be sure. I shut my brain to it, A-lahn, when I hear the far-away echo of that call."

"Have you heard it since I—came here?"

She shook her head.

Alan sat down deliberately upon the cushioned, swaying floor. He beckoned, and Evaya sank beside him in a descending billow of her pale garments and silvery clouds of hair. He was trying to keep a tight grip upon the spinning in his brain. There was so much to be learned, and perhaps so little time to learn it, if Flande was watching—if the enigmatic thing Evaya knew as a god were calling from its unthinkable citadel. . . .

"You've got to tell me—well, everything," he said. "From the beginning. Who are these gods of yours? Where did they come from?"

Evaya laughed on an exquisite ripple of ascending notes. "Not even Flande himself could answer all that! The gods? How should we mortals know? We have dim legends that tell of their conquering earth so long ago that we have no way to measure the time between. Great ships, dropping down out of the skies, bellowing thunder and flame. It may be they came from another—world—no one knows that now. They were beings from—outside. They wore light like a garment, and to them humans were—vermin. They cleansed the earth of them. And in the end, the legends say, they ruled earth from those citadels they had built, like the one above, keeping only those humans they had bred themselves, like us. To ornament their beautiful cities. I think Carcasilla is the only one left now."

Alan looked out over the airy suburbs floating before him, not seeing anything. Things were beginning to fit themselves together in his mind—but what stunning things, what appalling catastrophes and immeasurable vistas of time for a man's mind to encompass!

Earth conquered, ravaged, ruined—while he slept his timeless slumbers in the ship. The ship? A ship from space, like those the invaders must have come in? It was the inevitable answer. The being of the golden globe, the bodiless presence in the citadel, the questing thing at their heels in the mist, must somehow be one creature only—a Light-Wearer!

But what had gone wrong? Why had not the—the first of the alien beings—awakened when the armada that followed him came raging down from the skies? Why had this inhuman Columbus slept through the heyday of his race's power and glory, and wakened with his human captives only in the desolation of a time-ruined world?

Perhaps the Alien, first of his kind in a world inconceivably new to him, had misjudged the depths of his ageless slumber. His awakening, in the twilight of a dying world, must have been very terrible. Alan, from the depths of his own nostalgia for all that had passed into dust, could almost feel pity for the Light-Wearer who had come to lead his race to conquest—and slept, forgotten, while the dark sands of time ran irrevocably away. How frantically he must have scoured the empty earth before realization dawned that he was the last of his kind upon this ruined world. The first—and the last.

"Tell me about Flande," he said presently, in a controlled voice. It was not, he thought, wise to think very deeply on the subject of the Alien, and of Earth's ruin.

Evaya answered obediently, "Flande is very old and wise." (She was a toy, he remembered bitterly. A toy created of human flesh, to amuse the gods of earth. Obedience was bred into her from unthinkable aeons ago.) "Flande has never taken the sleep. None but he remembers all that has happened since Carcasilla's first days. He is afraid of forgetting, perhaps—something. He has many magics, and now he hates us both."

"Is he—human?"

"Flande is—" She paused, closing her eyes softly. And she sat perfectly still, the drifting hair settling about her shoulders. "You see—" she murmured, and lifted heavy lids with infinite slowness. "A-lahn!" she cried, with a curious, sleepy fright, looking at him under drowsy lashes. And she crumpled toward him, yawning with a flowerlike delicacy.

He caught her in his arms, and again he was vividly aware of her blown-glass strength and fragility.

"What is it?" he asked frantically.

"Flande—" she told him in a slow, drugged voice. "Flande—must be—watching. Listening to—our talk. He will not let me—tell you—about him. . . . I'm afraid, A-lahn—A-lahn dearest—the Light-Wearer. . . ."

She relaxed in his arms with the utter limpness of death itself, though he could still feel breath stirring her ribs gently against his arms.

So—Flande had struck.

Well, it had been as good a way as any, he supposed, to summon him into Flande's presence. This—this strange little whisper far back in his mind was not really necessary. He would have gone anyhow.

But it was not Flande who called.

Another voice—an alien voice—was summoning in the deepest depths of his brain. And beside him, Evaya stirred. "Yes, lord, yes," he heard her murmuring softly, in a voice entirely without inflection. "Yes, lord—it shall be done."

And she sat up stiffly. Her eyes were enormous, staring straight ahead, their pupils blackening the violet iris. Alan said sharply, "Evaya! Evaya!" and tried to shake her out of that mirror-eyed stare. She was as rigid as ivory under his hands. Even her face was ivory, not flesh, its delicacy frozen as if by some inward congealing of the mind. And she rose to her feet.

She went forward with deliberate steps. And Alan, bemused by Flande's power, could do nothing but follow, knowing with a dreadful certainty what was happening because of the stir deep in his own brain. . . .

So long as she remained awake and mistress of herself, Evaya had kept her mind closed to that distant call. But when Flande put his sleep upon her to stop her revealing words, he had opened the gateway of her priestess mind. . . .

Alan was scarcely aware of their passage through Carcasilla. That stirring in the roots of his brain blinded and deafened him to everything but the slim, cloudy figure moving stiffly on ahead, over the fantastic bridges, the spiraled streets, toward a distant spot which they both knew well . . . too well.

Before the great black circle where the light-veiled statue stood, Evaya paused. Alan paused behind her, a dozen paces away. The calling in his mind was very powerful now. A ravenous call, bellowing soundlessly from somewhere dangerously near.

Evaya touched something at the feet of the blinding statue, and quite suddenly a great flare of brilliance shot out all around the figure. It was like the blare of a struck gong, shivering out in a great wave over Carcasilla. If there could be such a thing as sound made visible, this was it.

Behind him, he heard the rising murmur of many soft voices, drawing near. All Carcasilla whispering its surprise, whispering perhaps with the awakening of memories buried deep behind the forgetfulness of many sleeps. Alan turned slowly and with infinite effort, for some inhibitory power was drugging his nerve-centers now and spreading through his body from that summoning in the brain.

The people of Carcasilla were answering the call. By tens, by scores, by hundreds, they came. Alan had not guessed before how many dwellers the city had. And when the last gossamer-robed citizen joined the crowd, and the wondering murmurs rose in a susurus all around them—exactly then, without turning, Evaya lifted her arms. Perhaps she touched some switch. Alan could not tell what.

She was facing the great circle of darkness upon the wall. Her arms were lifted, and her face. Her voice, clear and toneless as a bell, rang out over the assembly.

"Enter to your people, Light-Wearer and Lord."

A shiver seemed to run over the surface of the black disc on the wall. It was less disc than opening now. The opening to a long, dark tunnel. . . . Far down it something moved—brightly shimmering. . . .

Alan knew that it was infinitely far away. But it was rushing nearer with breathtaking speed. Each stride of its long legs—if these were legs—carried it shockingly nearer, as if it covered leagues with every step. The light-robes swirled around its devouring strides. . . .

It was near—it was almost upon them. It hovered, monstrous and glowing in the mouth of the tunnel, filling the high black circle of its disc. . . .

And then, with one great swoop, it burst into the violet daylight of Carcasilla.

Alan's confused impressions of the thing were too contradictory to have meaning. Was it monstrously tall? He could not tell, even as it stood there against the black mouth of the disc. Had it been blazingly robed in light against that blackness? He couldn't be sure. For, here in the light of the city, it was dark—a billowing darkness that swooped down upon its worshippers with a terrible avidity. It enveloped Evaya, who was foremost, in a cloud of nothingness, as if great unseen arms had seized her up in a devouring embrace.

Alan could not stir. His mind had congealed inside his congealed body, and he could only stand and stare, drowning in helpless wonder as he watched. For here at last, tangibly before him, was the nameless thing that had haunted all the hours of his awakening and the fathomless hours of his sleep. The questing creature that had run upon his tracks in the mist, the enigmatic watcher from the Citadel, the being whose dreams he had shared altogether too closely, in the long night-time of the ship.

He stared in frozen dismay as Evaya vanished into the cloudy grip of the Alien. Surely the Carcasillians had come to worship, expecting benediction—not this! This avid clutching grasp, as if the creature had been starving for countless centuries. . . .

Before the crowd about him could catch its breath, the tall, blinding robed figure—it was dark or light?—had tossed Evaya aside with a gesture almost of impatience, and was striding down upon the next nearest. It swooped and seized and enveloped with motion so incredibly swift that the Carcasillians could not have turned or fled even if they wished. And the great, striding god went through them like a reaper through grain, snatching up, enveloping, hurling aside figure after figure, and flashing on to the next.

Far back in Alan's brain, behind the helpless horror, the terrible revulsion, the more terrible taint of kinship with this being whose dreams he had known—lay one small corner of detached awareness. In that corner of his mind he watched and reasoned with a coolness that almost matched Sir Colin's scientific detachment. "It can't get at them," he told himself. "Somehow, they're protected. Somehow, the good Light-Wearers gave them armor to wear—like a spiked collar for their pets. Whatever it wants it isn't getting it here. Not yet. . . ."

The stooping and rising and inevitable nearing of that figure almost shook even the cool corner of his brain as it came closer and closer, reaping among the standing rows of Carcasillians. Alan strained vainly at his frozen limbs. Now it was two rows ahead of him. Now it was one— Tall, formless, all but invisible in its robes that were both lightness and dark. . . .

The towering, inhuman thing stooped above his head with an avid swoop, its robes fell about him like blindness to shut out the violet day. He felt a vortex of hungry violence sweeping him up. Vertigo—gravity falling away beneath him—

And then a strange, indescribable, long-drawn "Ah-h-h!" of inhuman satisfaction breathing voiceless through his brain. And a probing—eager, ravenous, ruthless—as if intangible fingers were thrusting down all through his mind, his body, among his nerves, into his very soul. They were bruising fingers that in a moment would rip him inside out, bodily and mentally, as a fish might be gutted.

Instinct made him stiffen against them, with a stiffening of more than muscles. His mind went rigid in anger and rebellion, along with his body. And the thing that clutched him hesitated. He could feel its surprise and uncertainty, and he struck out into the blindness with futile fists, gasping choked curses that were less words than anger made audible. He was awake now, vividly, painfully awake as he had not been since his first bath in the fountain. And he fought with all the fury that was in him against this devouring thing that was—he knew it now —starving with an inhuman hunger for the life-force he was fighting to protect.

This much he knew, in that inviolable corner of the brain where reason still dwelt. This creature was evil made incarnate, and its hunger was diabolic now. It could not touch the Carcasillians; he was its last hope. Its struggles to overpower him were as desperate in their way as his were to be free.

For one timeless instant Alan shared its hunger. And he shared its dismay and sorrow. He knew what it was to wake upon a dying world and find only the ruined relics of kinsmen that once had ruled the planet. Ruin and starvation and unthinkable loneliness.

He felt those gutting fingers thrust down along the track of the understanding thoughts, deep into his awareness, ripping and tearing.

He closed his mind like a steel trap against the treacherous sympathy of those thoughts, closed it as if he closed his eyes to shut out a terrible sight. With a brain tight-shut against everything but the danger he must fight, he stiffened against that probing, ravenous need raging all about him.

And he was holding his own. He sensed that. By fighting with every ounce of strength in him, he could hold his own. And when that strength began to fail. . . .

The blindness around him rifted now and again in his timeless, furious, voiceless fight. He could catch glimpses of violet light and the awed faces of the Carcasillians, and then dark again. Dark, and the starving desperation of the Alien tearing at him in a vortex of inhuman, demanding need.

And then, suddenly and bewilderingly—the bellow of gunfire.

That half-tangible grip upon him jolted—staggered —slipped away. Alan reeled back upon the slope of the white ramp, too dizzy to see anything clearly, knowing only in this moment that he was free and still alive. And then he heard—or was it a dream again?—a familiar, rasping voice, burred with strong emotion.

"Alan, laddie—gie us yer han'! Alan, here I am, laddie! It's Colin—here!"

Hard fingers dug into his arm, and a ruddy, bearded face, grinning with strain, thrust close to his. "Come awa', laddie—hurry! Can ye no see they're angry? Come awa'!"

Surprise had lost all power over Alan. Sir Colin's miraculous return from oblivion was not enough to startle him now. He wrenched away from that urgent grip on his arm, his mind taking up automatically what had been blanked out of it when the Light-Wearer swooped down.

"Evaya—" he said hoarsely, finding his throat raw, as if he had been shouting. Perhaps he had, in the blindness and silence of the Alien's embrace. "Evaya—"

He had seen her last lying on the white ramp in a

crumple of gossamer garments and showering hair. She was still there, but on her feet now, and looking down at him still with that face of inhuman ivory, the eyes blank mirrors that reflected only what the Light-Wearer whispered in her brain.

The Light-Wearer! Alan whirled, remembering, not feeling the tug upon his arm as Sir Colin rumbled an urgent warning. He could see the Light-Wearer at the very edge of vision, hovering cloudily down the slope. He did not dare look directly at it. The bewildering thing hurt his very brain as the eyes are hurt by brilliance.

It was the gunfire that had jolted it. He was still half in rapport with the creature from that terrible intimacy of the fingers prying down into his brain. He knew it was hesitating, torn between fear of the crashing thunder again, and that intolerable hunger still driving it on.

He could not bring himself to face it, but he knew when it decided what to do. He looked up at Evaya a moment before her toneless puppet-voice broke the quivering silence. It was the Light-Wearer who spoke, but the people turned to Evaya to hear the words it was putting into her mouth.

"Take them!" cried her voice, with a timber of inhuman fury in it that was not Evaya's. Her arm came up in a commanding gesture that carried a dreadful hint of hovering robes—as if her possession were so complete that even the garment of the Light-Wearer were visible around her. "Take them!" the inhuman voice thundered from her lips. (How hideous—how unthinkable—that the voice of a being not made of flesh spoke now through these lips of flesh!)

A low murmur of anger rose obediently among the

Carcasillians. They rolled forward toward the two men, blind, hypnotic fury on their faces. Beyond them the half-seen figure of the Light-Wearer shimmered like smoke upon the air. Alan could feel its thunder beating out at him.

One moment more, he hesitated. The memory of Flande had come back, and he was searching these blank, threatening faces before him. Was one of them Flande? Or was Flande human at all? Was he watching imperturbably through the showers of his raining tower?

"Damn ye, mon, wake up!" roared Sir Colin in his ear. "Ye aren't worth rescuing! Are ye comin' or aren't ye?"

Alan shook himself awake. "Yes," he said. "I'm coming."

The rising murmur of the Carcasillians sounded louder behind them as they hurried up the ramp. Alan hesitated with a moment's shuddering memory of the funnel of infinite blackness down which the Light-Wearer had come striding. The thought of entering it was worse than the thought of turning to face what lay behind him.

But when he looked, the tunnel was no longer there. The great round disc of the gateway opened now upon a passage of gray stone slanting away into dimness outside the violet daylight of Carcasilla's cavern.

Alan glanced back. Evaya lifted a face rigid as ice to him, a blind stare through which the Light-Wearer looked terribly into his eyes. Sir Colin called, "Hurry, mon!" in a voice that reverberated hollowly from the walls of the low passage outside.

Alan stepped through the gateway and out of Carcasilla.

Thunder bellowed from Sir Colin's gun as Alan cleared

the threshold. The noise was deafening; flinders of the stone flew from the corridor's walls as the air reechoed with the sound of the shot. Alan turned in bewilderment, to see the ruddy Scot's face of his companion wrinkling in a satisfied grin. "I thought so," Sir Colin said, lowering his gun. "Look."

A darkness was thickening over the doorway to Carcasilla. The violet light that poured through it dimmed as they watched, and within moments the barrier of darkness had closed over this gateway to shut them out, as the door of light they had first entered had closed to shut them in.

"It hates noise," Sir Colin grunted. "And it's still —maybe not sure of itself. I've had to use my gun on the domned thing before."

Alan did not at once realize the import of the words. He stared at the black circle upon the wall, a closed gate beyond which the Light-Wearer stood alone with Evaya and her people. He knew it did not belong there. The nameless builder of Carcasilla had put up barriers to keep out just such creatures as that. But now the dream-like city belonged to it, and the dream-like people, and Evaya whom he had known so briefly and so well—Evaya, the most dream-enchanted of them all, with her eyes that reflected the Alien thoughts and her body the instrument for Alien commands.

Sir Colin followed his gaze. "It's all right," he said. "The Light-Wearer can't hurt them. You saw that. But it could hurt us. We're lucky to get away so easily. I doubt if I'd have dared tackle *that*—that *thing*—if I hadn't seen it driven back by the Terasi's drums."

Alan looked at him, belated amazement welling up now that the crisis was over. The Scotsman had obviously been through strenuous activity since their parting. Scars and bruises showed through his ragged clothing, and there were new lines in his haggard face. But the red beard, unkempt and roughly trimmed, jutted with the same arrogant cocksureness.

"The Terasi drums? Those savages—how did you get away from them? And Karen—she's alive?"

Sir Colin patted the air soothingly with a big hand. "Karen and Mike are both verra much alive, laddie. But we'll talk as we go. And mind you keep a sharp lookout, too. The Way of the Gods isna so safe for men!"

"Way of the Gods?" Alan followed the Scotsman's gesture along the shadowy, ruinous corridor stretching before them. Once it might have been wider and higher, but it could never have been ornate, he thought. Now the broken walls gaped into the darkness here and there, blocking the pavement with fallen stones. "What gods?" he asked. "Why?"

"They call it that—the Terasi, I mean. And the gods were the Light-Wearers, of course. Didn't ye learn anything at all in Carcasilla?"

"I know that much, sure," Alan said, following Sir Colin over the broken stones that heaped the corridor floor. Here in the semi-twilight of ruin, Carcasilla's perfection seemed like a dream already. But it was hard to leave. He looked back over his shoulder at the closed black gateway upon the wall.

"It's the best way, laddie," Sir Colin said gruffly. "Come along. You'll realize that when I tell you what's happened. And keep your eyes open as we go."

"What do you expect?" Alan glanced uneasily about in the dimness.

"Anything at all. This was a—a sort of experimental laboratory for the Light-Wearers, once. The Carcasillians are one result. There were others." He nodded toward a gap in the wall, darkness within it. "*Something* used to live there, I suppose. And there, and there. Carcasilla's the last perfect experiment, but not all the others died at once."

Nothing moved but the rubble under their feet. But the dark doorways were numerous now, and Alan felt uneasily that things were watching as they stumbled over the stones. "What's happened?" he demanded. "Where's Karen? And Mike?"

"Back in the Terasi cavern, laddie."

"Prisoners?"

Sir Colin laughed. "No. At least—not Terasi prisoners. But I'm thinking we may all be prisoners of the Alien, my boy, and not quite realize it yet. . . . No, the Terasi aren't quite the savages they look. We found that out. It was our guns that saved us, you see. Not as threats or as weapons, but as a sort of promise instead. A promise of knowledge. They're hungry and thirsty for knowledge, these savages of the tunnels. So at first they kept us alive to learn the secret of the guns—how to make them, where they came from, why they work. They had to teach us their language for that. Ye've been missing a long while, laddie."

"You learned their language?"

"Enough. And now we're allies—against the Alien." He shrugged heavily. "Yes, we have a verra grave task ahead of us, laddie. The rebuilding of a world, perhaps. But we'll talk about that later. Here—we can go faster now."

The floor before them was a road of shimmering gray

metal. No, two roads, separated by a low curbing. Alan heard a rushing sound and felt wind drying the sweat upon his face.

"The Way of the Gods," Sir Colin rumbled. "Follow me now, laddie. Careful does it."

He stepped over gingerly upon the gray road. Instantly his heavy body rose weightless into the air, drifting forward as if upon the current of a slow stream. Over his shoulder he grinned and then beckoned. "Come!"

Alan braced himself and stepped uncertainly forward. He felt a giddy vertigo that nauseated him briefly. He shot past Sir Colin in the grip of the invisible air-river, and went dizzily along the tunnel, trying to right himself. Over and over, heels over head. Then Sir Colin's hand steadying him.

"Don't struggle. Relax now. There. The current's faster toward the middle."

"What is it?" Alan had fallen into a swimmer's position, head lifted, facing in the direction of the current's flow. Sir Colin drifted beside him. The tunnel walls moved past them with increasing speed, a soft murmuring of air in their ears.

"That gray stuff on the floor must cut off gravitation to some extent. Not too much or we'd smash against the roof. The force is angled forward, so we're carried with it. It's a river, Alan. A river of force. The Light-Wearers used it when they traveled the Way of Gods. It's one of the few things that still works in this god-forsaken place. This, and Carcasilla. . . . Tell me about it, laddie. What's happened since we left?"

And so Alan told him, drifting along over the gray ribbon of the roadway, through the ruins and darkness of the dead world. It did not take very long. Sir Colin was silent for a while as they floated on along the whispering river of air. Then, "Flande," he murmured. "I had wondered about him. Perhaps some day we'll learn the truth. But for the rest, it fits—yes, it fits verra well! I've learned a good deal since we came here, laddie."

"Tell me."

Sir Colin laughed and flapped his hands helplessly. "All at once? There's a lot to be said. Ye know about the Light-Wearers—how they came and conquered. How they cleared the earth of 'vermin' except for the pets they kept, and the experimental races they bred and interbred. Some of 'em—pretty nasty. And some of 'em still alive, the Terasi tell me, lurking in the caverns, feeding on each other and anything they can catch. I'd never realized *how* alien the Aliens were until I heard about the things they made out of human flesh in their laboratories here.

"But never mind that now. It's the Terasi ye'll want to know of. Back on their own world, wherever it may ha' been, the Aliens had a slave race. Not human, or even remotely human, but made of flesh like us. Not—well, vortices of living energy, or whatever the Aliens are. The slave race may ha' been the Aliens' hands. I'm theorizing, ye ken, but I've found out enough. And ye have to grant those Aliens were builders!" There was awe in the burring voice. "Anyway, when they came here they tried, I think, to make such a race from men. Parts of the brain they must ha' killed; others I believe they stimulated to make men builders, to be their hands as that other race had been. Only—they guessed wrong about humans. The little seeds of rebellion they thought they'd cut away kept growing back. Ah, those robot-humans built machines the like I never saw before. I'll show ye, later. I dinna know what for, but some day I'll learn. But the robot-humans learned something else, laddie. They discovered they were men!"

"Well?"

Sir Colin sighed gently above the soft sighing of the wind that blew along the Way of the Gods. "The Aliens destroyed them," he said abruptly.

Alan knew a sudden pang of loss, irreparable loss, as though history itself had become a book of blank pages.

"It may be," the Scotsman went on after a moment, "that the Terasi are remnants of that race. Or it may be they're descendants of some other experiments the Aliens made. There's been time enough to spare to let the human race rectify itself again from all the hideous things that Aliens superimposed upon them—if that's what happened. We'll never know, of course.

"The Terasi seem to be the only semblance of an independent human race left here. They're living in the great cave of the machines, where the robot-humans fought their last battles millenniums ago. And they're trying in their clumsy way to learn. Out of sheer thirst for knowledge, because there isn't any hope for the future and they know it well. The Earth's dying and the race of man will have to die, too."

He sighed again, heavily, and for a while they drifted in silence along the slow stream. The tunnel walls went past in the dimness, opening enigmatic arches upon caverns where the creatures of the Aliens must have lived out their misshapen lives so long ago.

"About the Light-Wearer—" Alan prompted presently.

"Oh. Well, he knows he's alone now, and he knows he'll have to die, too, if he can't get at us. We were domned lucky back there in the ship, laddie, that he didn't suspect then what had happened. He must ha' wakened and gone in search of the race he led here, and by the time he knew they'd come and ruled and died, we'd escaped. I imagine him going back to the citadel and sending out calls all over the world—and only Evaya answered. He followed us to Carcasilla—remember? He was still unsure then, I think, stunned by the shock of what he'd found here. And afterward, when he knew, he couldn't reach us. You were safe in Carcasilla, and we—well, the Terasi ha' found a way to keep the thing at bay.

"It isn' flesh, ye ken. Its metabolism isna human at all. It may have no body as we know bodies. So the bullets I fired didn't hurt the creature. No, I think it was the psychic shock of the concussion. It's a highly specialized being in which body had been sacrificed to mind. Perhaps a vortex of pure force. How can we conceive of such a being!" Sir Colin rubbed his forehead wearily, the slight motion rocking him upon the current of air. "Ye recall what happened back there when the devil attacked ye?"

Alan shivered. "It was in my brain—sucking—"

"So I think it's a mental vampire. It lives on lifeforce—mental energy—and only the energy of intelligent human beings. The Aliens may ha' bred human slaves for that purpose only. And now this last of them's ravenous—starving. And only we and the Terasi are available now. Ye saw how it cast aside the Carcasillians. They're protected, somehow."

"Well, the Light-Wearer came out of his citadel and went hunting. And he found the Terasi. And he came ravening among them as we saw him come into Carcasilla. But the Terasi have a weapon. They have great gongs that make the whole cavern shiver with noise. And noise those Aliens canna stand. Ye remember Carcasilla is a silent city? So they fight him with noise. He's been besieging them a long while now. We dare not leave the city without portable gongs, and even they aren't really powerful enough. The food-caverns—mushrooms and suck-like things—are a little way from the city, and we can't get enough now. He won't let us. We've starving each other out, really." Sir Colin grinned. "But I think the Alien may win."

"So you came after me alone?"

Sir Colin shrugged. "I had my gun. Besides, you saved my life a few billion years ago, in Tunisia, and I wanted to pay the debt. As for why I delayed—I did come once, and couldn't pass the barrier into Carcasilla. This second time I followed the Alien's track."

This was high courage of a sort Alan had seldom encountered, but he said nothing. After a while the Scotsman went on, "I may ha' done ye no favor in bringing ye out of Carcasilla, after all. It looks as if ye're doomed to starve with the Terasi, or die at last as ye so nearly died in Carcasilla to feed the Alien. I dunno, laddie. I think our fortunes lie with the Terasi, but even if we found a way to beat the Alien—what?"

Now the Way of the Gods grew wider, and chasms opened in the floor and cracks ran down the ruined walls. Sir Colin touched Alan's arm, drawing him out of the weightless current toward one of the broad splits running from roof to floor.

"Here's our way. There was a gateway into this cavern,

once, but a shrinking old planet like ours has its quake. That road's closed. Most of these cracks are blind, but some open in. Here."

Alan glanced on along the Way of the Gods still stretching ahead. "Where does it go?"

"Probably to Hell. I've checked it with what charts I could find—not many—and I think it begins under the citadel we saw back on the plain."

The scientist had produced a taper of some fibrous plant, and lit it. "We've got a hard path to follow."

It wound and twisted upward a long, rough way before light showed ahead, a cold, pale radiance outlining the mouth of a crack like lightning against a night sky. Sir Colin put out the torch. Before them, the depthless expanse of a cavern loomed.

Alan thought irresistibly of his first glimpse of Carcasilla. Here was a cavern again, and incredible shapes filled it. But this time those shapes were mighty cylinders and bizarre silhouettes rising like water-carved rocks from the sea. It was a city of—machines?

If these were machines, indeed, then the Alien concept of machinery was as strange as their concept of human houses in Carcasilla. What lay before Alan was too vast, too breathtakingly immense, to be captured in familiar terms. These towers were machines perhaps, but of a size inconceivable! Only Alien-made metal—or was it plastic—could create such masses that would not topple under their own weight. And they were colored gorgeously and senselessly. Deep colors for the most part. Gargantuan shapes of purple and dark wine-red, and leaning towers of obsidian green.

"Aye," breathed Sir Colin at his elbow. "They were

technicians!" There was respect in his voice. And Alan remembered that this cavern had seen perhaps the last rebels of earth, robots turned stubbornly human, fighting and falling before their Alien masters in a saga of courage and futility that was lost like the race that had failed. Only their handiwork remained, enigmatic, impossible.

"What are they for?" he asked Sir Colin futilely. "What *could* they be for?"

"What does it matter now?" the Scotsman said bitterly. "There isn't any power left in the whole domned planet. Come on down. It's not so safe up here."

They mounted a lip of rock, and the rest of the cavern floor was visible below them, a twisting rift of stone leading downward toward it. Against the farther wall Alan could see a huddle of rough huts—more like partitions than like shelters, for what shelter from the elements could men need here? Figures were moving among them, and Alan bristled a little involuntarily. The savage shapes looked dangerous; he could not forget his last meeting with these people.

Before them, shadows stirred, and for one breath-taking instant Alan was back on the shore of the Mediterranean, where Mike and Karen had come out of the Tunisian night with their guns upon him—as they came now.

No one spoke for a moment. There were lines of strain on Karen's keen, pale face, and the blue eyes held an habitual alertness he had seen there before only for brief moments of violent action. Her bronze curls were tousled now, and her clothing tattered, with inexpert mends.

Mike's had not been mended at all. He stood there

straddle-legged, a menacing figure of strong bronze, his blunt features restrained to an impassivity more revealing than any scowl. There was an air of iron firmness and strain about him. The sleek black head was roughened now, and he had the beginnings of a black beard. He looked taut as wire—and as dangerous if he should break, Alan thought.

Karen was watching Alan. "So, Drake, you're still alive."

"We all are," Alan said with a glance at Mike.

"You look damn good," the gunman remarked coldly. "Somebody been feeding you well, eh?"

Alan's mouth quirked. "I haven't eaten anything since I left you."

"Where's Brekkir?" Sir Colin asked.

"In the storage house, checking supplies," Karen told him. "Food's pretty low. If we don't send out another party soon to the food caves, it's going to be too late."

Sir Colin shook his head, lips tight. "I want to talk to Brekkir. Come along, laddie. Ye'll remember Brekkir —the man who stove your ribs in." And the Scotsman smiled grimly.

"I remember." Alan nodded, ignoring Mike's sudden bark of vicious amusement. There was still, he recalled, a score to be settled with Mike Smith. But not yet.

Under the great toppling heights of the machines they went, mountains of purple and rich deep blues and greens. Dead machines. But whatever air-conditioners had been installed unknown years ago were built for the ages, because the air was fresh here. Windless, but cool and clean. And the dimming lights shone down unchanging.

"What about you?" Karen was asking now. "The Alien—"

"I've met it," Alan said briefly.

Mike showed his teeth. "What is this Alien, Drake? Scotty's been talking about energy and vibration, but it doesn't make sense. The filthy thing can be killed, can't it?"

"God knows." Alan shrugged. "Not by bullets. It's afraid of sound, apparently, for whatever that's worth."

"But it can be killed!" The sentence was not a question. White dints showed in Mike's nostrils. The Nazi had courage, Alan knew for a certainty, but never before had that courage been tested against the unknown.

Mike's years of training with the German war machine had given him certain abilities, but it had destroyed certain others. Nazi soldiers fought to the death because they believed they were the master race, the *herrenvolken*. It all seemed trivial now, and incredibly long ago, but in this one application it was not trivial. For Mike had the weakness and the strength of his kind. When the German supreme confidence is undermined—that fanatical, unswerving belief in one's self—the psychological reaction is violent. And Mike Smith, brave as he undoubtedly was, had for weeks been facing a power against which he was completely helpless.

Over his shoulder Sir Colin said brusquely, "The Alien's not a devil. It's alive, and it has adaptability—to some extent. Without perfect adaptability it's vulnerable."

"To what?" Karen murmured.

"Metabolism, for one thing. Without food it willna live."

"Comforting!" Karen said. "When you think that we're the food it wants!"

Alan saw Mike Smith shudder. . . .

"Hungry?" Sir Colin asked as they came into the huddle of Terasi village under the out-curve of the cavern wall.

"Why, yes. I am. Thirsty, too." Alan felt surprise as he realized it. In Carcasilla the fountain had been both food and drink, but here he was mortal, it seemed. And he was not only hungry, he was famished. And very tired. That fight with the Alien had been more draining than he had realized, until now that comparative safety was reached. He was scarcely aware of the rude streets they were walking, or of the ragged Terasi who passed with curious stares, or of the great gongs hanging at intervals along the way, manned by grim-faced watchers.

Weariness and hunger made the whole cavern swim before him as reaction set in. He knew that Sir Colin was helping him into some rough-walled house, its roof only a network of pale-branched trellis. He heard Mike and Karen from far away. Someone put a spongy bread-like object in his hands and he tore at it ravenously, remembering the Alien's hunger with a wry sympathy now as he ate the mushroomy thing in his hand.

It helped a little. Sir Colin poured water into a metal cup and handed it to him, smiling. "There's no whuskey," he said gravely, "which probably accounts for the downfall of mankind."

The water was sweet and good, but food and drink were not all his wants now. He felt drained dry of energy by that terrible bout with the Alien. And he knew—he sensed unerringly that the Alien was not yet finished with him. He could feel it in the back of his mind as he ate and drank. Somewhere it was waiting, watching. . . .

"Sleep now," Sir Colin urged from somewhere outside the closed circle of his weariness. "We'll wake you if anything happens."

He did not even know when gentle hands led him to the bed.

IV

THE PORTALS OF LIGHT

A DEEP, resonant vibration, shivering through the room, wakened Alan. He lay there staring, uncertain where he was. The sound came again as he lay blinking, and this time he recognized it and sat up abruptly, lifting one hand to his stubby cheek. The beard was beginning to grow again, as it had never grown in Carcasilla. But he had no time to wonder over that, for the gong was ringing desperately now and the whole cavern seemed to resound with that ominous sound.

Alan was halfway to the door when Sir Colin came in, grinning.

"False alarm—we hope," he said, and cocked his head to listen. The gonging vibrations died slowly outside. "How d'ye feel this morning, laddie?"

"Better—all right. But that gong—"

"A sentry thought he saw the Light-Wearer shimmering in one of the crevices. That was all. He started an alarm, and the others are watching. Ye'll know soon enough if the thing's really there. D'ye feel like meeting Brekkir this morning?"

"Brekkir?" Alan echoed. "The leader, eh? Sure, bring him in. Is it really morning?"

Sir Colin laughed again. "How can I tell? They measure time differently here. Brekkir's waiting outside. I'll call him."

He stepped to the door and lifted his voice. A moment later Karen and Mike came in, nodding briefly to Alan's greeting. Behind them a great ragged figure entered. The same tattered savage, magnificent as an auroch in his breadth of shoulder and tremendous depth of chest, who had come charging up Flande's spiral waterfall with terror and determination on his hideously scarred face. The same shouting barbarian whom Alan had last seen above him, driving his heels down crushingly into Alan's ribs.

A glint of sardonic humor gleamed in the man's deeply recessed eyes. Alan braced himself warily as the Terasi came forward and put his great hands on the other's shoulders, stood back at arm's length to scrutinize Alan with a look of wonder growing on his harsh face. He said something to Sir Colin in a deep-chested gutteral.

The Scotsman answered, nodding toward Alan. When he had finished, "Brekkir wonders at your recuperative powers," he translated. "He says he gave you mortal wounds."

"I'd have died, all right," Alan said grimly. "It was the fountain that saved me."

Sir Colin gave Brekkir the words in his own tongue. The Terasi's shaggy brows lifted. He pushed aside Alan's shirt and ran calloused fingers along the healed scars that banded his torso. Excitement shook his voice when he spoke again.

The Scotsman answered, and he, too, was excited.

Karen broke in to ask, "A power source? What does he mean?"

"I'm not sure. But this is something I hadn't expected, though I should have guessed from what Alan's been saying. If Brekkir's right, we may have the answer to all our problems. Though it seems incredible!"

Alan stared. "What is it?"

"I'd best show you on the scanners. There's so much to explain. Look—Karen's brought your breakfast. Eat it while Brekkir and I talk."

Alan let himself be pushed down to a seat before a makeshift table of plastic blocks, and Karen set more of the mushroom-bread before him, and a cup of water. She was watching Brekkir's scarred face, bright with a sort of triumph, as he argued vehemently against Sir Colin's cool questions. Mike watched, too, though obviously the flurry of quick discussion was a little beyond him. Strange, thought Alan, how little they had changed in these weeks apart.

But it was not wise to think, somehow. For so long he had been half-asleep, his mind dulled, living in the incarnate dream that was Carcasilla. His thoughts felt strange now. It was difficult to believe in the reality of anything that had happened. The act of independent thinking was like resuming the use of a paralyzed limb. His brain did not feel entirely the brain of Alan Drake.

He had the curious illusion of seeing through the wrong

end of a telescope. Brekkir was a tiny figure gesticulating to a microscopic Sir Colin. He saw them with objective coldness, as if they were beings of a different species.

Deep in his mind a furtive, cold horror stirred. But far down, smothered under clouds of lassitude, Alan's awareness of *himself* faded. His own body seemed alien, no part of his consciousness. And a slow desire was rising in him that had no kinship with human passions. It was in his mind, tiny and far away, and then leaping forward with great striding bounds, as the Light-Wearer had come from the Way of the Gods.

It was hunger he felt, that deep and terrible desire —ravenous hunger for—what? Hunger, and beyond it a desperate solitude. He was alone. He was wandering in some formless place, searching amid great ruins that breathed out desolation. And the hunger grew and grew.

He heard Sir Colin's voice faintly; the sound was unpleasant. It grated on his senses. He struggled against the grip of strong hands whose touch was hateful.

"Alan! For God's sake, wake up!"

But he was awake—for the first time. This creature was trying to stop him from returning to Carcasilla. That was it! He must go back! Only there could he find appeasement for this dreadful hunger that burned him. He must go back to the Light-Wearer, open his mind—but no, he *was* the Light-Wearer; Alan Drake was the willing sacrifice.

"Karen!" the burring, alien voice called again, tiny and distant. "Mike, help me hold him! He'll kill—"

And Mike Smith's strained voice. "Let him! Let him go! The Alien's here—I can feel it! Those gongs were right. It's come, it's here in this room!"

Then Karen's swift steps racing across the floor and her

hard, small fist cracking savagely against Alan's jaw. Blaze of pain; flashing lights. Then a timeless eternity of groping, a frantic striving for orientation. The world steadied. Sick and weak, now, from reaction, Alan saw an altered world—a normal-sized Sir Colin flung aside by a towering Brekkir who charged forward with shoulders hunched, eyes hot and deadly.

It was instinct that showed Alan the gun at Karen's belt. He was not yet wholly back in his own mind, perhaps, but his body thought for him. The metal was cold against his palm. He swung the pistol up unwaveringly at Brekkir while the room lurched around him, knowing only that if he revealed weakness now he was gone.

"Hold it!" he snapped, hearing his own cold voice still a little alien to his ears. But he was himself now. The possessor was gone. And it must have shown on his face and in his impassive eyes under the full lids, for Brekkir paused, reading danger in the voice he could not understand. A second of indecision, and then Brekkir shook himself and stepped back, his breath coming in heavy, uneven gusts.

"All right, Karen?" Alan asked without looking at her. "Will he—"

"I don't know. Sir Colin's the only one who can handle him. Whatever happened, it was bad."

Mike Smith licked dry lips. "It was the Alien. He was *here*. He was *you*."

Sir Colin got painfully to his feet, came forward to put an arm about Brekkir's great shoulders. The Terasi muttered, shaken. Sir Colin answered briefly.

"Gie me yer gun, Alan. He docsna trust you. It's all right now, but gie me the gun."

Alan laid it in his outstretched hand, hesitating a little. Brekkir seemed relieved, but his smouldering eyes still brooded upon the other. Sir Colin said:

"All right now, laddie? Ah-h. But—God mon! What happened? Ye were—were—"

Alan sat down heavily. "I'm all right now. But I could stand a drink."

"Hold hard." Sir Colin's grip steadied his shoulder. "Let me see your eyes. Yet. . . . But for a while they were all pupil. Black as the mouth of Hell! I'll admit, ye've shaken me. But I think I know the answer."

"You do?" Alan moistened his lips. "Then tell me."

"It was the Alien, laddie. Ye are verra, verra sensitive to that creature. Like a bit of iron sensitized by a magnet. It may pass. I trust it will."

Alan pressed his palms against aching eyes. "It's like being possessed of a devil."

"It is that! Ye maun fight it, then. If it can control ye from a distance—yet ye fought the thing in Carcasilla."

"I hope to God it never happens again," Alan said in a shaken voice. "The worst part was that I—I liked it. I lost all sense of personal identity." His teeth showed in a furious grin. "I—let's not talk about it just now."

Sir Colin glanced at him sharply for a moment, then seemed satisfied. "Aye, but Brekkir—"

At the sound of his name the Terasi glowered and muttered something. Sir Colin nibbled his lower lip. "Brekkir fears ye, laddie. Or rather fears your falling under the Alien's control. It's like having a spy from the enemy in your camp. Ye'd better stick close to me. I've promised Brekkir I'll keep an eye on ye."

A voice shouted from outside. Brekkir listened, then grunted to Sir Colin and hurried out. The Scotsman grunted in turn. "Come along, all of ye. Trouble, as usual. And a good thing for you, Alan; it'll give Brekkir something else to think about!"

They hurried through the Terasi village, where ragged savages shrank away from Alan with loathing in their eyes. Evidently rumor had run fast through the town. But the gongs were not booming now, which was one small comfort. The Alien had withdrawn—for a time, and for its own purposes. They were to know in a moment what those purposes were.

Sir Colin led them at Brekkir's heels around the base of a vast leaning tower of deep-green plastic and in through a sloping door in its base. Spiral stairs rose steeply. They were all dizzy with the rapid turns before they came out into a domed room high above the cavern floor. A sort of frieze ran about the circular wall, head-high, divided into foot-long rectangles of cloudy glass. Beneath each were several wheels like safe-dials. Most of the screens bore decorative designs, but the one before which Brekkir stopped showed a picture.

A picture of Evaya!

Alan pushed closer, staring. He seemed to be looking down upon the scene, and from one side. The screen was full of motion now—full of the men and women of Carcasilla, streaming along the Way of the Gods, their faces glowing with fanatical exultation. And Evaya walked before them, her lovely pale hair drifting upon the air-currents, her face blank with the blankness of her possession.

"A television plate in the passage," Sir Colin's precise

explanation came. "This is the scanner room, Alan. It connects with thousands of viewers scattered through the caverns, many of them not working any more, of course. Watch."

Brekkir spun a dial; a new scene showed—the Way of the Gods, bare and empty. Far away along it, motion stirred. The swirl of gossamer robes, pale faces crowding. And then—striding with great swooping bounds, robed in darkness and in light, in fire and cloud—came the shape that no eyes could clearly see. Leading the Carcasillians strode their god, the Light-Wearer.

A shock of dismay shook Alan. He felt Brekkir's shoulder beside him heave convulsively. Mike Smith made a hoarse, wordless sound deep in his throat.

"Logical," Sir Colin said quietly, as though he were lecturing at Edinburgh. "I should have foreseen this. They have no weapons yet, but I don't doubt *It* knows where to find weapons."

"What are you talking about?" Mike snapped. "Is it coming here?"

"Certainly. Where else? It wants food, and we are its food, not the Carcasillians. It can't pass our sonic protection alone, so it calls in the Carcasillians as an attacking force, to silence our gongs if they can. After that. . . ."

Brekkir barked an order over his shoulder. One of the Terasi in the room went out swiftly. Brekkir pulled at his beard and eyed Sir Colin. The Scotsman grunted.

"Less than a hundred Terasi, but the women can fight, too. The Carcasillians—how many, Alan?"

"Several hundred, I'd guess."

"They'll be no match for us, alone. But depend on it, they'll have some sort of weapons when they get here."

Alan turned his mind from the sickening picture of the delicate doll-army from Carcasilla falling beneath the bludgeons of the Terasi. But he knew he could not protest. The Terasi were right. Even Evaya's blown-glass loveliness was a vessel for the Alien now—a vessel to be shattered.

He would not think of it.

Brekkir grunted something behind him, and Sir Colin nodded.

"Forget that now. Tell me about the fountain, laddie. All you remember. It's important."

"There isn't much to tell." Alan frowned, remembering.

"It's still alive? Still powerful?"

"Well, it healed me. And it gives the Carcasillians immortality."

Sir Colin spoke to Brekkir, who fumbled with the dials.

"Here's the story, laddie. Listen now, it's important. Forget the Carcasillians while ye can. It may be we've got the solution right here in our hands—if we live through the next few hours. This rebel race that lived here in the cavern was a sort of maintenance crew for the Way of the Gods. It kept the worlds alive along it. So we have these scanners and other things. It's a library, too. There are visual historical records. I'll show you, presently. Mind you, this is important. Because the Aliens told their slave-race how to maintain the underground worlds. Gave them too much knowledge, perhaps, for they never expected revolt. And when the revolt came, the slaves died, as I told ye. But the records remain. Look."

Under Brekkir's blunt fingers a picture flashed upon the

screen. Alan watched with less than half his mind. He could see only the Carcasillians, blind and helpless and deadly dangerous, marching on the Terasi.

But as the pictures changed on the screen he found himself watching involuntarily. The world's surface, smooth and lifeless, slid past in panorama. He saw gigantic ruins, like nothing man's world had ever known. He saw death and desolation everywhere.

Once, he caught a glimpse of the great abnormal asymmetries of the citadel lifting against a misty sky, and curiosity suddenly burned in his mind about what lay inside it, but he knew he would never learn that now.

And once he saw the flash of a deep gorge, bottomless, vertiginous, its far side hidden in fog. And far away along it a moving white wall that drew nearer. Alan thought of a flood bursting down a dry arroyo. But this chasm was immeasurably vast, and the flood was deluge. Prismatic rainbows veiled it. Boiling, crashing, and seething like a hundred Niagaras, now, the mighty tide swept toward them, brimming the chasm.

Alan felt a faint tremble shake the floor. Sir Colin nodded.

"The sea-bed—what's left of it. The moon's verra close now, and its drag is tremendous. In a million years, it's cut a gorge across the planet. This is all that remains of the ocean. It follows the moon around the earth."

"That thunder we heard when we first left the ship," Alan remembered. "That was it?"

"Aye. Watch."

Vision after vision shifted across the screen. Desolation, ruin. And yet there was life here. Gigantic worm-shapes slid through the mists, and once one of the flying half-human things drifted down the slopes of air above the tidal chasm.

"No intelligence," Sir Colin murmured, pointing. "They follow the water and eat weeds and fish. They are no longer human."

More scenes changing on the screen. Gray dust, gray death. . . . And then, unexpectedly, a forest—green, lovely, veiled in silvery fog. A shallow pool where a fish rose in a ring of widening ripples. A small brown animal raced out of the underbrush and fled beyond the scanner's range.

Alan leaned forward, suddenly sick with a passion of longing for the past he would never see again. Green earth, lost springtime of the world! He could not speak for a moment.

"It is the past," Sir Colin said gravely. "A part of history, but a history we never saw. Perhaps a thousand years ago, perhaps more. It is the planet Venus."

"The Aliens went there?"

"Aye. But they didna stay. No human life to feed them. They came back to earth and died here. But do ye na see it, Alan—Venus is habitable! Humans could live there!"

"A thousand years ago—"

"Or more—nothing in the life of a planet. We have records of the atmosphere on Venus, the elements, the water and food. Humans can live there, I tell ye, laddie! And now, perhaps will!" He lifted bony shoulders. "If what we hope is true. And if we live to prove it."

It was Karen who answered.

"The Aliens destroyed their space-ships, toward the end. Used up the metal for some other purpose, maybe, or maybe for the energy in them. For a long time the Terasi have known they could live on Venus if they had a ship and a power-source. Now there's a ship. The one that brought us here."

"Well, the ship's big enough to carry us all—Terasi too, I think. We could go to Venus and rebuild the race on a new world. *If* we had any power."

"It is a second chance for mankind," Sir Colin said gravely. "But—no power. No power in all the world. The Terasi checked that long ago. Only little scraps like those that keep these scanners going. Till I saw you, Alan, I had no idea that there might be a power-source left on earth."

"The fountain!" Alan said.

"Aye. The Terasi knew no Carcasillians until you came. They never guessed about the fountain. But there it is, and there must be a source to keep it burning. Enough to take a ship to Venus! That I know." Sir Colin struck a gnarled fist into his palm. "I have searched and studied here, and I'd stake my soul on that. If we could only take it out—power the ship with it!"

"What is the source?"

"I dinna quite know. Radioactivity, perhaps, yet something more. The Aliens brought it with them from the stars, and it's a strange stuff. I know a little from charts the robot-humans left here. A glowing little nucleus that consumes itself slowly and sends out radiations. Will ye bet there isn't one of them under that fountain in Carcasilla?" His voice shook as he spoke.

"That fountain—the Carcasillians live by it," Alan reminded him slowly.

"Aye, a sterile life. They'll never rebuild civilization. But the Terasi, now—they're strong enough to face hardships on the new world. And they have fine minds. If we could get back to Carcasilla—we canna be sentimental about this, Alan, laddie. That may be the last power-source on earth, and we maun use it to save mankind."

Alan nodded without speaking. Yes, they must take it if they could. There was nothing the Carcasillians could do to prevent them. All over the city, that violet light dying, the fountain of life fading, the delicate folk who were made for toys tasting mortality at last—hunger and thirst and death. The bubble city shivering in the cold winds from outside, its floating castles shattered, its colors dimmed. And Evaya in *the gathering shadows—Evaya, with her eyes blank mirrors, through which the Light-Wearer stared!*

Alan said harshly, "All right. What's the plan?

It was Karen who laughed. "The plan? Why, keep the gongs going while we can, until the Alien breaks through and gets us." Her voice was brittle.

Sir Colin said evenly, as if she had not spoken, "The plan would be to get back into Carcasilla, I suppose—now, while the people are gone—and try to find what lies beneath the fountain and see if we can use it."

Alan said suddenly, "Flande! Flande won't be gone! Flande's no fragile toy for the Light-Wearer to command. And the Carcasillians aren't quite as helpless as we thought, not while Flande's alive. He'll prevent our taking away the power source, if only for his own safety!"

"Aye, Flande," Sir Colin said heavily. "I'd forgotten him. Flande's a force I haven't reckoned with. He's too enigmatic to fit in anywhere until we know who he is, or what. But Karen's right, laddie." The big shoulders of the older man sagged.

"We've got another problem here and now," he said,

then. He nodded toward the screen upon which the flutter of gossamer garments was passing. "They must be nearly here. The Alien's making his last bid, you know. He'll have something—"

The brazen note of a gong thundered out from the cavern below them, cutting off his words. The echoes spread shuddering through the whole great space of the cave, and another gong answered them, deeper-toned, vibrating. And then another. A diapason of quivering metal, like the striking of shields, rose and bellowed and rent the air within the cavern with a mighty crashing.

Mike's hand went to his gun. "This is it."

Brekkir sprang to the stairway. They followed him dizzily upward, around and around, until the sloping roof opened before them. Far below lay the machine-city and the cavern floor.

The deafening vibrations of beaten metal roared out, echoing and re-echoing from the walls and the arched roof. Around them, on roof-tops, in the streets, knots of Terasi were gathered about heavy plates that gleamed like brass. Crude sledges swung and crashed with resounding force against the gongs.

Booming, roaring, bellowing, the Terasi thundered their defiance to the last of the living gods.

Brekkir pointed. In the cracks that split the cavern walls, figures stirred. Pale figures, gossamer-robed. The Carcasillians, clambering like hundreds of ants above them.

Mike jerked out his pistol and fired, but Karen struck down his arm.

"Hold it! Save 'em, Mike. We haven't got too much ammunition."

Mike looked at her, paling. Karen shrugged. Then she looked up quickly as a thin lance of light shot down from the distant cavern wall. It touched a platform nearby, where Terasi were swinging their measured blows heavily against the bronze plate.

The Terasi jumped aside, startled. But the ray did not seem to harm them. It went through their bodies like x-rays made visible. But on the surface of the metal it exploded in white fire. Broke there, and crawled, like a stain.

The Terasi lifted their hammers again and struck savagely. No vibrating thunder followed the blows. The gong clanked dully, like struck lead.

Sir Colin grimaced.

"Heat-rays that don't harm living organisms," he said.

"What is it?" Karen asked.

"After a bell's been heated in a furnace, it won't vibrate. Same principle, I think. The Carcasillians can silence every gong here with those. See, there goes another. Now, where the Alien found such weapons, I'd give a lot to know."

"You won't know," Mike told him, with a faint echo of hysteria in his voice. "We'll never know. Look—another gong has gone!"

The worst thing, thought Alan, was the fact that the heat-rays did not harm human flesh. The Alien was saving his humans alive.

"And we can't *do* anything!" raged Karen, striking the rail before her with both hands. "We've even got to save our ammunition for the noise—or for each other."

The delicately colored carriers of doom were creeping closer now, ignoring the Terasi arrows. Now and then Alan saw one find its mark and a gossamer-robed denizen of the city that never knew death fell silently among the rocks. But the Carcasillians crept on, and long fingers of light went probing out before them, seeking and silencing the gongs. That tremendous swelling bellow of sound still rioted through the cavern, but just perceptibly it was lessening now. One gong, or two or three, made no real difference that could be measured. But the toll inevitably was mounting.

Helplessly Alan watched the fragile army advance. How incongruous it seemed, that these doll-like creatures could bring doom upon the savage Terasi, creeping down the walls in their floating garments, firing as they came. Evaya would be somewhere among them, fragile and lovely and blind. Unless an arrow had found her already. . . .

(It had been like holding life itself in his arms, to hold that resilient steel-spring body, so delicate and so strong. He had been near to forgetting that latent strength in her, which would never matter to him now. He thought of the dizzy moment of their kiss, while the bubble city rocked below them. He must forget it now and forever—for whatever time in eternity remained.)

And he knew that this way of dying was perhaps as good as any, and easier than some. For now he would not have to watch Carcasilla shattered and ruined and dark.

Also, he knew, suddenly, as he heard the gongs falling silent one by one below him, that he would never have left Evaya in a dying Carcasilla while the Terasi set sail for the future, even if Flande had let them rob the fountain of its power. He knew he would have gone back to the ruined city and taken that fragile, resilient body in his arms and held her, waiting while the darkness closed around them both.

In the end, he knew now, they must have died together, one way or another. This was quicker and so perhaps it was easier.

He looked up and saw a pale shimmer far back in a chasm of the walls, and a hard shudder of revulsion shook him. Easier? Easier to die in the Light-Wearer's terrible embrace?

He watched it, fascinated, glimmering far back in the darkness, waiting and urging its puppets on.

The pale light lanced down from all around them. And the cavern was no longer bellowing with shaking sound. Here on the roof-top they had no need to shout to one another any more. Alan saw Karen take a firmer grip upon her gun, saw her shoulders square beneath the ragged blouse.

"Well, it won't be long now," she said grimly. "This is it, boys. Too bad—I'd have liked to see Venus."

This had happened before, Alan thought. And it had happened in his own lifetime—in the familiar world of the Twentieth Century, before an unguessable flood of years had swept him to the end of time. Below the sloping rooftop where they stood watching, the little army of the Terasi stood at bay, their bull thews and savagery useless now against the weapons that struck from far away, fingering out like swords of living light.

In the past such scenes had happened many times. In Tunisia, he remembered, at Bataan and Corregidor, wherever the armadas of sea and sky and land had met in conflict, such hopeless battles had been fought. But this, he thought, was the last battle of all.

These were civilization's last defenders—these brutish, iron-bodied men—and this little group of less than a hundred represented all that he had known of the world that was gone. The towers of metropolitan New York, the gray cathedrals of London, the white ramparts of Chicago lifting above the blue lake—these were the symbols of a race that built and aspired—a race that had gone down to defeat.

All over the earth was darkness. Civilization's last sparks were being crushed out here, where mankind fought savagely and hopelessly on its last remaining fortress. The thunder of the brazen gongs was fading imperceptibly as the heat rays licked out to splash in white fire across them.

Alan glanced around at the tense little group on the rooftop. Sir Colin, a tattered, scarecrow figure squinting down at the battle with a look of cold, impartial, scientific interest on his face. Mike Smith, half-crouched, hand nervous on his gun, his quick eyes raking the walls where Carcasillians moved like gaily colored moths in the crevices. Mike was afraid. Not of the Carcasillians, not even of death—but of death in the embrace of the terrible shadowy thing that waited in the darkness, watching.

Karen—he had respected her even in the long-gone days when she had been in the German espionage, and he an American Army Intelligence officer fighting her with every weapon he knew. It seemed ludicrous now to think in those meaningless terms, but he realized suddenly that she had never been intrinsically a Nazi; she was an adventurer, playing for high stakes and ready to take the consequences if she failed. Yes, he could respect Karen. There was a suggestion of a grim smile on her face as she met his glance.

Alan did not think of Evaya. She was up there somewhere, a slim, fragile, steely creature who was no longer human. And she would accomplish her inhuman purpose very soon now, and the demon that possessed her would come sweeping into view, leaping like a hound to the kill, ravening with the hunger of a million years.

The arrows of the Terasi still lanced up toward their besiegers. Now and then a Carcasillian fell, gossamer garments streaming, to death on the rocks below. And death was so new, so strange to these toy-like immortals from an immortal city led by the fountain of life! The city fed by—power!

And power would save the Terasi—if they could reach it. If it were not as hopelessly far away as power on another planet.

Save them? Would it?

What was it Sir Colin had said about great mechanical gongs, built by the rebel race to fight the Light-Wearers? Alan reached out suddenly and gripped the Scotsman's shoulder.

"Those gongs," he said in an urgent voice. "The big ones. Where were they?"

Sir Colin gave him an abstracted glance. "Inside the machine towers. Some of them underground. Why? They were power-driven, remember. You can't—"

Alan struck the parapet triumphantly. "If we had the power, then, the heatbeam couldn't reach 'em! Sir Colin, I'm going to get you the power!"

The Scotsman's face came alive, but with a startled distrust that surprised Alan.

"Anyhow, I'm going to try. We can't be worse off than we are right now. The gateway to Carcasilla's open now—you saw that in the scanner—and nobody's left there but Flande. There must be a way back from here that wouldn't lead through the Carcassillians. Tell me what to look for and I'll try the fountain."

The distrust on Sir Colin's gaunt face had changed to a desperate sort of hope. "You're right, laddie. It's worth a try—by God, it is! But we'll have to hurry."

"We?"

"I'm going, too."

Mike shouldered forward, sweat shining on his bronzed cheeks. "So am I."

Sir Colin frowned. "Your gun's needed here, Mike."

"The hell with that! I'm not going to stay. That—that *thing*—" He broke off, showing the whites of his eyes as he glanced up at the crevice where a pale shimmer flickered now and then as the Alien urged its puppet army on.

"There's no assurance we may not meet it ourselves," Sir Colin said dryly. "Still—Karen?"

"I'm staying. I can help here. Fighting's one thing I know a little about."

"Good lass." The Scotsman touched her shoulder lightly.

Brekkir, watching their sudden animation in bewilderment, grunted something that only Sir Colin understood. They spoke together in gutterals. When the scientist turned back to Alan his ruddy face was alight with new enthusiasm.

"Brekkir says there are ways out, if we're reckless

enough to leave the noise of the gongs. He'll find us a lead box, too. We'll need something to carry that—that dynamite-pill without the radiation destroying us all. What the thing is the good God knows, but I suspect something like a radioatomic energy—perhaps a uranium isotope. . . . Aye, it's a risk, lads, but think what it means if we win!"

The timeless current that flowed whispering along the Way of the Gods swept them weightlessly toward Carcasilla. They talked little, in hushed voices, as they drifted through the dimness. Alan thought of Karen, pale under the tousled red curls, saying good-by at the tunnel entrance. They might never meet again. He thought of Evaya, moving like a soft-winged moth against the craggy walls, blind and terrible, raking the Terasi village with a beam of death. He thought of the way light kindled behind her exquisite features when she smiled, like an ivory lantern suddenly glowing. He thought of the springing resilience of her body in his arms. And he knew that there was no risk too great to face if it might mean her awakening.

"I'll come back," he thought grimly.

And then he remembered that if he did come back it meant the end of Carcasilla and Evaya's death. So he stopped thinking at all, and gave himself up to watching the violet circle of light that was Carcasilla's open gateway grow larger and larger and larger up the tunnel before them.

They were stumbling over the broken pavement toward it, beyond the sweep of the air-flow, when Alan was briefly aware of a sudden rocking of the world around him. Values shifted imponderably; he was not himself any more, and these men beside him—these tiny, nameless creatures. . . . He must have made some hoarse, inarticulate sound, for Sir Colin's hands were suddenly heavy on his shoulders.

"Alan! Laddie! Wake up!"

Everything turned right side up again with a sickening dizziness. In the dimness Alan blinked at the scientist.

"You're all right now, aren't ye, laddie? Answer me!"

"Yeah," Alan muttered, his tongue feeling numb. "It—caught me by surprise. Gone now. I—" He glanced back along the tunnel. Nothing. . . . Or was that a flicker of light, far away, almost invisible? Light that was somehow darkness, dark that blazed with supernal brilliance? It was gone as he looked. "I can fight it," he said. "Don't worry. We know I can throw it off if you help me. But for God's sake let's hurry!"

And so, with Sir Colin on one side gripping his arm, and Mike on the other breathing heavily and fingering his gun as he shot ugly glances sidewise, Alan came back into Carcasilla.

The bubble palaces, the flying avenues still hung like colored clouds in the air, but they were empty and silent now. It was strangely like homecoming to Alan Drake. He knew each spiraling ramp so well, each cluster of floating globes. And nostalgia struck him hard with a double impact—once for the lost Evaya with whom he had walked these airy ways, and once for the ruin he must visit upon this lovely city if he succeeded in his mission here.

V

THE ALIEN'S EMBRACE

DIRECTLY BEFORE them loomed the great statue of the Light-Wearer, enigmatic, robed in blinding brilliance. One thing that he saw beyond it brought a cold thrill of foreboding. A soaring crystal bridge that spanned an arch above the statue was shattered half-way across its curve, as though the hammer of Thor had smashed ruthlessly down on Bifrost. Sir Colin's gunfire! That was it! The bullet or the concussion must have shattered that vibrant arch.

Silence brimmed Carcasilla like a cup. Before them through the bubble domes the violet fire of the fountain rose in brilliance toward the mists of the cavern roof. And under the fountain—power. Power to drive back the Enemy and save the last indomitable remnants of civilized mankind!

"What's that over there?" Sir Colin asked in a puzzled voice. "Flande's tower, but—"

Alan knew where to look for that pinnacle of running rain poised incredibly on its spiral of stairs like waterfalls. He squinted through the clustering domes.

The tower was not there. A cone of light flamed in its place. Lambent radiance like moonlight.

"The gateway when we first entered Carcasilla," Sir Colin rumbled. "Remember?"

Alan had a brief, poignant recollection of Evaya's slim Artemis body silhouetted against the golden disc that had shut out the following Alien.

"It can't pass those shields of light," he said aloud. "Flande's built himself a barrier somehow, out of the same stuff."

Sir Colin jerked his head in agreement. "Guid enough. As long as he's shut up there, he won't be troubling us. Now the fountain—is this the shortest way, laddie?"

"That green street, I think, between the purple globes. Here, I'll show you."

They went up the winding avenue in a silence so deep that their footsteps sounded abnormally loud. Instinct made them keep their voices hushed as they wound along through the airy labyrinths aglow with delicate color. And the color, curiously, seemed to vibrate until Alan's eyes could scarcely make out the way. What he could see looked wrong.

Mike said, "We're taking a hell of a long time to get there, seems to me," and shot a wary glance across his shoulder. All of them had been doing that. Alan muttered some reassurance that did not sound very confident even to himself as he led them up an undulating boulevard through rings of floating spheres. Behind him, formless and intangible, he could feel the shadow of menace shaping itself like fog rolling together.

The blinding vibration of color clouded his eyes. They were striding faster now up the undulant street, almost running.

Vision suddenly cleared before Alan's eyes. At their feet the city dropped away, spread out below Flande's tower! He stood with Mike and Sir Colin at the foot of that cone of light which veiled the tower of rain. But he *knew* he had been leading them straight toward the fountain. . . .

Low laughter shook through their minds. Flande's laughter. Words were forming there, but before Flande could shape an intelligible thought in their brains, Mike choked on a shout and flung up a pointing arm. Alan turned to look.

The image of the Light-Wearer still blazed against the opened Gateway. But something was wrong. There were *two* figures now—and one of them was no statue.

Blinding in its darkness and its light, tall as the fountain itself—the Alien stood in the threshold of Carcasilla.

Then it leaned forward and leaped toward them with gigantic strides. It moved with such dazzling speed that Alan could not even try to focus its inhuman image. A paralysis of terror held them motionless on the platform. Nearer it came, and nearer, covering incredible distances with each soaring stride.

And then like a shroud dropping noiselessly around them, a dark curtain shut out Carcasilla.

In the sightless blackness Sir Colin's voice said levelly, "It's Flande, I think. He's saved us—for the moment. Wait."

The scrape of flint-and-wheel sounded, and a wavering point of fire sprang into life on the Terasi device he carried. In its yellow flare they could see what looked like a wall of water rushing soundlessly down just before them—the surface of Flande's tower. Alan found his voice, surprised that it was steady.

"That's it, all right. It can't get at us now."

"You're sure?" Mike Smith's voice shook. It was infinitely harder for him to admit defeat than for the others. His tough integrity was crumbling almost before their eyes.

Alan turned toward the wall of rain, and said, "Flande, Flande!"

In response a luminous slit began to glow in the wall. The veils of water parted slowly. Light shone out through a swirl of rainbow mists, dissipating the dark in which they stood.

Then Flande's face, immense, god-like, hung suspended in the great oval. Through his endless vistas of memory Flande looked out at them again, young-old, immortal, infinitely weary. And yet Alan thought he sensed a change. Beneath that passionless coldness pulsed something new, something vital, like . . . Alan thought: *Fear. It's fear*.

Within their minds Flande's telepathic voice rustled like leaves in a soft wind.

"The Light-Wearer cannot break through. You are safe here."

"You—saved us?" Alan asked incredulously. "But—"

Mike broke in. "How the hell did you get us here,

anyway?" His voice was belligerent. Flande had humiliated Mike once before, and the memory of it thickened his anger now.

Flande's remote, impersonal gaze touched the gunman.

"Hypnotics, of course, fool."

"Of course," Sir Colin echoed, tilting his head back until the red beard jutted as he looked into Flande's face searchingly. "The question is—why? Ye weren't so friendly the last time we met."

"It is for me to question—not you," Flande told him austerely. "Answer this—has the Light-Wearer fed yet?"

A broad grin cracked Sir Colin's bearded face.

"Och, that tears it!" he said. "So that's why he saved us, eh? So we wouldn't be food for the Alien? Yes, I'm beginning to understand. The Alien can't harm the Carcasillians, but he can harm *you*, or you'd not protect yourself like this. Ye've been hiding here."

Alan half expected the flaming sword of radiance to flash, but it did not come. Flande looked down in quiet silence. After a long while he said, "All that is true enough. But we are both food for the Light-Wearer, and you will do well to treat me with respect."

"Is it still there?"

Flande paused, his eyes going unfocused with a look of inward searching. Then: "No. It is leaving now. It goes back along the Way. It knows it cannot penetrate this veil. . . ."

His voice in their minds trailed off. And then he shot a sudden question at them with the impact of a shout: "Why did you come back?"

"To ask your help," Sir Colin answered, quickly and smoothly. "To join forces in fighting the Alien."

"You lie," Flande said in a cold voice. "When you lie, I know it. Furthermore, the Light-Wearer cannot be destroyed. Surely you realize that."

"You're wrong," Sir Colin flashed back, as though he were correcting a recalcitrant student. "The basic laws of physics and biology must apply to everything on this planet, and life, being energy, is subject at least to entropy—by which I mean the Alien *cannot* be invulnerable. It fears sound, anyway."

"You hope to conquer it with noise?" Flande's voice was contemptuous.

"We've held it at bay with noise, at any rate."

Flande's brows lifted. "Indeed? Tell me about it."

Sir Colin hesitated. "No harm in that," he said at last. "If we're to join forces I suppose ye'll have to know what's happened. Here it is."

Quickly and concisely he recounted what had been taking place in the cavern of the Terasi. When Sir Colin had finished, Flande's face hung motionless, the lids lowered. Then with surprising suddenness the lids rose and a furious blaze of anger lighted the eyes beneath.

"So!" Flande's voice burned in their minds. "You will lie to me, will you? Stupid human fools! Did you think I was not aware that you were heading toward the fountain when you reentered Carcasilla? All I needed was the knowledge of where you'd been—and now I know. You come from the cavern of the great machines, useless for want of power. You came back to the only source of power left along the Way of the Gods. You even carry a box of lead. Do you think I need ask why?"

Sir Colin shrugged as the thunderous anger beat away to silence in their brains.

"So now ye know. What next?"

Cool detachment dropped once more over Flande's angry face. The lids drooped.

"I need not gamble. Here in my tower I can wait until the Light-Wearer starves."

Alan gave a harsh bark of laughter. "You'll have a long wait. It'll reach the Terasi soon, and there are nearly a hundred of them."

"No matter. I can sleep. When I waken it will be another century, and the Light-Wearer will be dead."

"Maybe," Alan said. "Maybe not. You won't be able to get to the fountain. Without that you'll die."

"No, I shall be in catalepsy; my body will need no fuel. By the time I waken only the Carcasillians will be left alive."

"Your shield here—won't that fail if you go into catalepsy?" Sir Colin asked.

"My shield is the power of the mind," Flande said, with a touch of pride. "As for you—"

"Yes, what about us?" Mike Smith's voice was rough with tension.

"You must stay, too," Flande went on as if Mike had not spoken. "Stay and die, I suppose. If I left you free, you might find some way to rob the fountain. And certainly you would go to feed the Light-Wearer, and thus postpone still further the hour of my awakening. No, you must stay. But your death will be easy. I shall put my sleep upon you."

A ribbon of silver fire flashed out above them. It coiled like a snake, winding into a net of intricate fiery patterns. They glowed on Alan's retina, burning deeper and deeper, into his very brain. He could not wrench his gaze away.

Sir Colin whispered hoarsely, "Hypnotism! Dinna look at it, Alan—Mike—"

The ribbon of fire coiled on. Mike's breathing grew thick. There was no other sound. Sir Colin's hands fell away. . . .

There was nothing in the world but that serpentine silvery ribbon, writhing into shapes of arabesque brilliance. Symbols—words in no known language. Alan could almost read their meaning. But not quite. It was the language of dream.

Hot agony seared his shoulder. With slow reluctance he retraced the steps back toward consciousness. The burning pain was relentless. It dragged him back. And now he could move again. His gaze jerked downward to the taper lying at his feet, its wick fading into a coal. Its burning had broken the spell.

When he looked up again the silver ribbon was gone. And except for that dying coal the darkness around him was complete. Flande had closed his door, retreated into the slumber that would last a hundred years.

He heard hoarse breathing at his feet. He stooped. Mike and Sir Colin lay motionless in the grip of hypnotic sleep that would end only in the deeper sleep of death. He shook them hopelessly.

Alan straightened in the darkness, facing the unseen wall through which Flande's passionless face had pronounced doom upon the race of man. If he could waken Flande, perhaps the barrier around the tower might fall. And if the Light-Wearer swooped through to devour them all—well, the Light-Wearer was winning anyhow, and even that was preferable to death without hope.

How had Evaya summoned Flande, long ago? Alan stepped forward in the darkness, arms outstretched. Three steps and then the cool surface of the wall met his hands. He pressed. Nothing happened. He shifted his hands and pressed again. Still nothing. Did it work only when Flande willed it? He moved his hands once more.

A tiny slit of light glowed in the dark, spindle-shaped, expanding like a cat's pupil. Rainbow mists were curdled beyond it. And beyond them hung the face of Flande, immense, immortal, eyes closed in a slumber like death.

Alan's full-lidded eyes had narrowed to shining slits. There might be sorcery inside this tower—but death was coming to meet it.

He stepped through the colored mists and into Flande's doorway.

The great face still hung before him, its eyes asleep. But the force of gravity had shifted strangely. He thought the floor was no longer underfoot, that he was dropping faster and faster toward that silent, enigmatic, gigantic face hanging in the gray air. The mists, he saw without surprise, were gray, too, now, and thick between him and Flande. And drowsiness was mounting about him as though he breasted a rising tide. The sands of sleep, too light to fall, hung in suspension inside Flande's tower.

He stood at the threshold of the Face. It loomed like a cliff above him. He struggled forward, heavy-limbed, against the tide of sleep—and stepped through the illusion of the face.

Beyond it was grayness again, and sleep that beat at him with great, soft, stunning blows—like bludgeons of cloud. . . . Another step forward, and another—remembering Evaya—

There was no face. Perhaps there was no Flande? There was nothing at all but sleep.

His knee struck something resilient and soft. Moving in a dream, he leaned over, and with an incredible precision that could happen only in dreams, found his hands fitting themselves about a throat.

The hands tightened.

Violet light pouring down around him wakened Alan from a dream in which he knelt with one knee upon a yielding couch and strangled a being who lay there. The mists of sleep were fading from his brain. He blinked. He stood in a great peaked tent of rain. Its soundless torrents poured down all around him along the walls, translucent, with the violet day of Carcasilla glowing through.

Then the barrier was gone!

He looked down. And he knew it was no dream. This was Flande's face purpling upon the couch, the same face that had hung in gigantic illusion in the doorway. But a man's face, a man's perfect, deathly white body stretched upon the couch. Flande's eyes looked up into his, wide, shocked into wakefulness, still veiled a little behind the memories of infinite time. But the layers of withdrawal were fading swiftly now, as ice cracks and melts, and Flande was lost no longer in the memories of his thousand years. It was no god whose throat Alan gripped—but a strangling man.

Flande's face was blackening with congested blood, red veins lacing the whites of his staring eyes. He would be dead in another second unless—

Alan let him drop back on his cushions. Flande lay still for a moment, coughing and choking, pawing his throat with soft, pale hands. He was, Alan saw now, neither

Carcasillian nor Terasi. Perhaps his race had died millenniums ago in some little world long the Way of the Gods. His body was symmetrical as a Belvedere—but soft, incredibly soft. Alan thought he knew why. A thousand years of inactivity, of stasis—Flande's muscles must have changed to water!

A sound beyond made him turn. The curtains of rain still swayed apart to show Carcasilla through the opening. Sir Colin was clambering in now, a little dizzily. Behind him peered Mike Smith.

"The Alien?" Alan asked swiftly.

Sir Colin shook his head. His voice was thick. "I looked. Nothing—yet."

Alan told him what had happened, watching his keen little eyes rake the interior of the tower even as he listened. Wakefulness was making his bearded face alert again by the time Alan had finished.

"So—" murmured Sir Colin, with a sharp glance at the still coughing Flande. "He's no such a god now, eh? And this place of his empty. I wonder. . . ." He moved across a floor like still, depthless water, to examine the farther wall. Mike followed him uneasily.

Flande's coughing lessened. He was sitting up, now, on the couch. His eyes, fixed on the doorway and on Carcasilla beyond, were wide and filled with terror. He saw that the barrier was down.

"Stop him!" Sir Colin's hoarse cry echoed from the walls of rain. Alan leaped forward, but his leap was a fraction of a second behind Flande's. The soft body hurtling against his shoulder spun him off balance and he saw only a pale flash as the deposed godling shot by him toward the door. Mike Smith whirled, a grin of savage pleasure on his lips, and dived for the flying figure. His hand grazed Flande's ankle; then he was stretched face down on the smooth pool of the floor, mouthing deep curses. Flabby Flande might be, but he could run!

Mike scrambled up. The three of them jammed for a moment in the doorway. Then Mike broke through and sprang down the waterfall steps, tugging at his gun.

"Don't shoot!" Sir Colin called. "We need him!"

Then they had no more breath to call. The spiral steps seemed to whirl underfoot as Alan followed the scientist's flying heels. When they reached the level Flande was far ahead, a pale figure flashing among the crystalline buildings, Mike's dark bulk pounding in pursuit.

The chase led along the rim of an abyss that dropped away to swimming distances. Sir Colin's age began to tell before they had run a hundred steps. Falling behind, he motioned Alan on.

Alan, rounding the edge of a great eggshaped dome, saw that Flande was heading for the fountain. From here they could see it gushing up out of its basin, a great pillar of violet fire. Flande and Mike, dodging among the buildings below them, were drawing nearer and nearer to the wall of glassy multicolors above which the basin loomed.

Flande reached the wall. Alan could see the flash of his terrified white face as he worked frantically at the wall. Mike Smith plunged toward him, head down. Then suddenly there was an arched opening twenty feet high gaping in the wall. Across its threshold stole a faint, quiet light that had in it something of the fountain's radiance. Alan could not see what lay inside.

He heard a thin, high-pitched wail of despair and looked

up to see Mike hurling himself forward at Flande, hands clawing out. Briefly their bodies struggled. Then Alan saw that Mike had the demigod by one arm, twisting it viciously, a savage light of triumph on his face. He said something Alan could not hear.

"Easy, Mike," he called, hurrying down the last stretch of blue ramp toward them. "You'll break his arm."

"Yeah, that's right!" Mike grinned fiercely at him over one shoulder. "What about it?"

Flande, on his knees, was beating unavailingly against his captor's hand, a stark, unreasoning horror in his eyes—fear, thought Alan, that did not involve Mike Smith. Instinctively, he glanced back toward the Gateway, but its great circle stood empty in the wall.

Sir Colin came panting down the ramp.

"Mike!" he snapped. "Ye'll have the mon fainting on us! Ease up now, like a guid laddie."

Reluctantly Mike obeyed. He hoisted Flande to his feet, but kept a tight grip on the flabby wrist. He said contemptuously, "I could kill him with one hand."

"No need now," Alan said, with a queer conviction that he spoke the truth. "Flande can't use his magic. Hell, he isn't even using telepathy!"

It was true. Flande was pouring out frantic syllables in the trilling, birdlike tongue of Carcasilla. There was no trace of that vast calm on his face now; the demigod had collapsed with a vengeance, leaving only a very terrified man in his place. It was hard to believe that the giant visage which had awed them so in the doorway had any connection with this babbling creature in Mike's grip.

"Let me go!" he was crying now. "Quick! Quick, before it comes!"

"Calm down," Alan said. "It isn't here now. Maybe—"

"It will come! It knows the force-shell is gone. It will come swiftly now!"

Alan said, "What's beyond there!" and nodded toward the archway behind Flande.

The demigod averted his face stubbornly, not answering. Mike twisted his captive's arm ruthlessly. Alan said nothing. This was no time for half-measures; anything was justified that gained an answer which might help them.

After a moment Flande cried out shrilly, "Stop him! Make him stop! I can't stand this—"

"What's inside the arch?"

"The—the power-source. I swear it! Now free me!"

"Why?"

Flande licked dry lips. "Look," he said abruptly. "If I tell you this, if I save you from the Light-Wearer, will you free me? Otherwise, we die together here, when it comes."

"All right," Alan said. "What's the answer?"

"Let's go inside—"

"We're staying right here until you talk." An unpleasant chill was crawling down Alan's back at the thought of the Light-Wearer flashing toward them along the Way of the Gods. But he dared make no concession to Flande. He nodded at Mike, who applied a little more pressure. Flande cried out.

"I'll tell you! But we must be quick. *It*—"

"*What's inside?*"

"The power-source that gave me my magic," Flande said, talking fast. "I came to it long ago, when I first found Carcasilla. This place is forbidden. None of them dare enter. But I dared, and I saw the birthplace of the fountain." His voice changed timbre a little. "I saw the Source. You've bathed in the fountain—you know what it can do. It healed you when you were dying; it gave you immortality. But *I* have seen the Source! *I* have stood at the outer edge of its radiance and bathed in the terrible glory of that power. . . ." His voice trailed away. Then he said simply, "It made me a god."

"How?" Alan demanded curtly.

Flande gave him a burning look. "How could you understand? I have stood closer than any human creature ever dared stand to the heart and the source of immortality. Here in my body and my brain there dwells something of that same power now. The brain of man has many secret chambers—their locks flew open before the impact of that force and I knew—I saw—" Again his voice died. Then, wearily, "But I am drained now. Building the force-shell was harder than I knew. Now I must bathe again, to replenish the power. Let me go—let me go, and I will build the shield around us all."

"What's he saying?" Mike asked impatiently.

Alan told them in quick sentences.

"The Source is down there, all right," he finished. "But it sounds like something too dangerous to tackle. If the mere radiation of the outer edges did that to Flande, what actual contact with the thing itself would do I—"

Flande's flat, thin scream broke off the sentence. Their eyes followed his shaking finger.

At the top of the long slope, against the background of

the city and of Flande's pale tower of rain, something moved. A formless shape of shadow and blinding radiance, impossibly tall, and horribly graceful in its swift, stooping motion. Eyelessly it watched them.

Mike's reaction was shocking. He seemed to fall in upon himself, like an old man; a palsy of terror shook him, and the bronze face relaxed into a mask of imbecile fear.

Flande's thin squeak roused them from their paralysis. He twisted free from Mike's flaccid grip and spun toward the tunnel behind them, moving fast.

The motion had an almost hypnotic effect on Mike as he whirled away from the terror above them. Here was a soft, frightened, fleeing thing—a thing that had offended the man's pride and must be punished. Mike redeemed his terror of a moment ago in headlong pursuit of this creature which feared him. He flung himself after Flande with a hoarse shout.

Some premonition of what Mike intended galvanized Alan into action as he saw the Nazi's first forward stride. Flande must not die yet. Alan hurled himself against Mike Smith's shoulder with all his weight, sending the Nazi staggering. Before Mike could recover, Alan was sprinting down the tunnel after Flande.

The tunnel slanted sharply down. Flande was a flying white shape outlined against golden brilliance as he plunged down the slope. Alan could hear the pounding feet of the others behind him and for an instant wondered horribly if he could hear the Alien's footsteps, too, as it ran upon its nameless limbs.

To flee from a thing that could move with the Alien's flashing strides was worse than futile—yet they ran. And except for Mike, perhaps, they ran more from the Alien itself than in pursuit of Flande.

Then Alan came without sight of what lay at the tunnel's foot, and for a moment all memory even of the terror behind was washed away. For a great room opened before him, brimming and blinding with a radiance he could not face. The eye could not measure the room's size, for distance was warped and distorted here by the light that glowed in great rippling beats—from the Source.

Pure light had poured into these walls so long that even the rocks glowed now, translucent, permeated through and through with the strength of that golden violence. The walls were windows opening upon glowing distance; they were mirrors that gave back and refracted the light upon its Source. The whole room swam with it, so that Flande's white figure, forging desperately ahead, seemed to advance against great waves of brilliance that beat *through* him as he ran.

In the center of the room a corona of light danced around the dazzling glory of the Source. Directly above it a circle of darkness drank in the swirling tides of energy. The fountain, then, must rise directly above this pool.

Toward it Flande was plunging, against intangible waves he had to fight like waves of strong wind. But he had slowed his pace.

He was glancing over one shoulder now, at his pursuers, at the tunnel beyond which the Alien must still be hovering. Now he had reached the outer circle of the corona and he paused there, hesitating between the danger behind him and the burning danger ahead. Farther than this he had never dared to go.

Alan paused, too. The light was blinding, and he was

not eager to come any nearer to that boiling heart of energy at which he could scarcely bear to look directly. Silent tongues of pure golden fire leaped out around it, and the room swam with the power of the Source.

Flande stood hesitating in that bath of flowing radiance. And Alan thought that a change was coming over the demigod's face. A strange deepening of his eyes, as if godhood were distilling in his brain from the Source that burned beyond him.

Mike's hoarse shout behind him broke the spell. Alan heard Sir Colin cry out something unintelligible in the rolling echoes that woke along the cavern walls as Mike plunged shouting past him, brushing Alan to one side with his momentum, blind to everything except the presence of his quarry.

Alan's own voice rose in a useless cry, mingling with the echoes that rolled from the radiant mirrors of the walls. Mike hurtled past him, head down, a black bulk in the cavern of luminous sunlight. In silhouette Alan saw him stretch out both hands in unseeing, heedless triumph.

Flande screamed, his voice strangely deeper and more resonant. There was a thud of body striking hard against body. Alan, squinting against the brilliance, could see them toppling, locked in an embrace of rage and terror, while the silent flood of sun-rays breathed rippling past them.

They fell together, Flande and Mike Smith, into the heart of the boiling maelstrom that was the Source.

For the beat of a second Alan could see them standing there together, still locked in that furious grip, while the pure, pale violence of the flame burned blindingly through their bodies. They were shadows against that light.

Shadows that ceased. The light barely flickered. Its serene waves beat out from that heart of fire.

And Alan stood alone in the golden cavern. . . .

Sir Colin's heavy footsteps hurrying down the ramp broke the trance a little and Alan turned an unseeing face toward him. His mind was still too stunned to accept what had just happened. He stood in dumb incredulity, seeing the blaze burn on, radiant and powerful.

"God!" breathed Sir Colin softly. His face was drained of color. He must have seen enough to understand what had happened.

Then something flickered beyond Sir Colin's head, and Alan stirred a little in his daze. He could look up the length of the tunnel from here, seeing a circle of Carcasilla framed in the opening, Flande's tower shining in its center. And he could see something else—something that shimmered and swirled like blindness at the tunnel's threshold.

"Sir Colin," he said, in a voice that did not sound like his own. "Sir Colin! The—Alien's come!"

The Scotsman's eyes shifted blankly from the Source's blaze to meet Alan's look. The bony shoulders moved in a shiver, and Sir Colin drew a long, shaken breath.

"Ah-h," he said, and his voice was strange, too. "The Alien. And we canna run any farther now. Mike may ha' been luckier than we." He turned. "Aye, I see it. But look, laddie! It isna' comin' in! I wonder—"

Alan looked, steeling himself to face the sight of that robed and terrible shape. It stood hesitating in the tunnel mouth, moving forward a little, then moving back, almost as if it were afraid.

"Could it be the Source it fears?" Sir Colin wondered aloud. "I doubt it. The Aliens themselves must ha' brought the Source here. I'd say it's much more dangerous to us than to—It. Poor Mike—"

"Forget about Mike now," Alan said shortly. "Later we can think about that. Now—"

"Ye're right, laddie." Sir Colin's shoulders squared. His voice was coming alive again, now that he had a problem to solve—and solve quickly. "There must be a reason it's hesitating—there must! But I canna think it's the Source. Och, if I only had more time! That Source! With it, I think we could defy even the Alien, there. But we'll need shields and tools. The thing in the fire's too much for the like of us, barehanded. There's a core of something in that basin. God, if we had the time! But that *thing* out there—"

"It's coming," Alan told him in a level voice, looking up. "The tall shimmer of blindness was stooping down the passage toward them now. Hesitating, peering at them without eyes, retreating a pace or two—then coming on with that terrible, unearthly grace to devour them.

"It's afraid," Sir Colin said behind him in a quiet voice. "Something about us worries it. Now what? *What?*"

There was something in that calm question that made Alan rally even in this moment of hopelessness. How great a man this was, who could speak so coolly while death marched down upon him! Sir Colin, knowing himself the helpless prey of a being that had already wiped earth nearly clean of human life, could reason quietly as he watched death come stooping down the tunnel toward him.

"It's weakened, you know," Sir Colin murmured, squinting up at the shimmer in the tunnel. "It's starving. Perhaps it's weaker than we think. It's growing more desperate—and yet warier, at the same time. Now what—why—"

"Got it!" said Alan, and sudden hope made his voice shake. "The gun! The noise! Don't you remember?"

"It's afraid of sound, aye. But what good will—"

"This cavern isn't so big. Fire a gun here and—you think it can reason that well? Does it know what echoes gunfire would raise? I know how it drew back and vibrated and waited when you fired at it by the gateway."

Sir Colin's eyes were squinted under the tufted red brows. "I'm getting it. The Alien's a thing of energy, a matrix of electronic forces, perhaps, held in a certain rigid balance. Vibration upsets the balance. Aye—the concussion of gunfire might hurt the thing enough. But it'll only run back and wait for us at the tunnel mouth, where the echoes wouldn't be so loud."

"You think the concussion might actually disable it, if we could hold it here in the tunnel?"

"There's a chance, laddie. The thing's afraid of something. It may be that. But we canna hold it. I've thought of everything under the sun—" He laughed. "I've even thought of bathing in the corona back there and turning demigod like Flande. But Flande was domned afraid o' the Alien, too, ye'll remember. So that's no help, except—" He looked down at his gun.

"I can hold the Alien," Alan said. He spoke so softly that he had to repeat it before Sir Colin heard. Then the keen little eyes under the red brows pierced at him like needles. The Scotsman shook his head slowly, lips compressed. "Ye canna mean that, laddie. The Source and the fire are a better choice than that. Or—" He glanced down again at his gun.

"It's a chance," Alan said stubbornly. "It's worth the risk. We can't lose more than our lives. I'd rather burn like Mike and Flande, if there were no hope. But there is! Listen now. The thing out there's dying of hunger. Give a starving man food and he'll hang onto it even if you use a whip on him. I saw that done once, in the Sahara, by Bedouins. And—well, this time I'm the entree. The whole damned course. But the Alien will have to pay for what he gets!"

"No, laddie. No!"

"Don't forget, the Alien's been in my mind before. I fought him off, with your help. Maybe we can do it again. Don't argue. Get your gun out!" He spun toward the passage where that shape of terror burned white and black, wavering toward them in its blindness. "This is it!" Alan said. "I'll be right back. Get ready!"

He ran up the tunnel with long, easy paces—not giving himself time to think. Feeling was frozen in him now and must remain frozen until—until the Alien was destroyed.

The thing towering up the tunnel before him stooped, suddenly, in his direction, a shape of blindness he could not focus upon. Blinding light and blinding dark, breathing out hunger in monstrous, tangible waves. It moved one long stride forward, its robes of light and darkness swirling against its limbs.

Alan did not even see it move as it cleared the space between them. One second it was stooping toward him, tall against the outlines of Carcasilla. Then in an avid leap it seemed to grow to gargantuan size, hovering above him, folding down in a canopy of blindness.

Smothering, in an embrace so engulfing that he could not see nor feel nor think, there was awareness of those terrible gutting fingers that thrust down into his mind and soul, shaking with eagerness in their ravenous need.

And he knew in that moment that he was lost.

VI

HEIRS OF THE SHATTERED CITADEL

SUCH POWER swirled and slavered around Alan as he had never dreamed existed. The Alien had not exerted its full strength in their meeting by the gateway. It was a strength as great in its way as the sun-blaze of the fountain's source, and he could not hope to match it with any power he possessed. This was a being from beyond the stars, a being whose race had swept man like vermin from the earth. Fighting it was like defying the lightning.

He could not do it. He had misjudged himself and his adversary, and he was lost. Sir Colin was lost, and the Terasi, and all mankind. The consuming blaze of the Source would have been an easier way to die. Or Sir Colin's gun.

Crashing thunder bellowed all around him. Gunfire doubled and redoubled in echoes that rolled along the walls. And the Alien, shaken by the impact, relaxed its thrusting fingers for an instant. Briefly, sight returned to

Alan. He felt a shudder go rippling through the force that held him. For a timeless moment as he felt it withdraw, he watched emotionlessly the course of Sir Colin's bullet. A soaring bridge crashed tingling into ruins. A bubble dome flew into rainbow fragments. And he saw the stairway spiraling upward toward Flande's tower spring into sudden vibration that shook the whole precarious structure until it blurred. Distant sound of it rang thinly in his ears. He saw the spiral shatter as slowly as a dream, saw the great streaming tower begin to topple.

Blindness closed down on him again, in one monstrous swooping rush. And there was anger in the violence now—a cold, iron anger as inhuman as the stars, as if the Alien understood what had happened, and why.

Hopelessly Alan stiffened against the force of the ravenous desire that whirled to a focus upon him again, boring down into his consciousness with irresistible fingers. In the one corner of his mind that was still his own, he remembered that he must somehow drag this cyclone of terrible power back down the tunnel. A man dragging a typhoon would be no less impossible. Even if that man had the full power of his own will—and Alan's will was going.

He could feel it falter. And dimly, from a source without, as if he were two awarenesses at once, he could feel curiously strengthened. It was as if a hollow within him had begun to fill.

Rage shook him—a curious, icy, inhuman rage, its cold flame turned upon the little human creatures who were fighting to deny their meaningless lives that had no purpose except to fill his need. *His* need. *His* burning, insatiable desire. He must hurry quickly, quickly out of this tunnel where that agonizing vibration could shake him to the heart. But agony or no, he would not give up now. Not with consummation so close in his embrace.

Blinding rainbows of pain shot out around him, through him, like widening circles of fire. There was noise, concussion. Unbearable weakness for a moment loosened every synapse in his being.

Through dark veils Alan saw the tunnel sloping down toward that corona of brilliance. Sir Colin, dark against it, leaned peering forward, gun poised, face contorted painfully with strain and terror. For one instant their eyes met. For one instant Alan was himself. He heard the echoes of the gunfire go rolling along the corridor, heard a faraway, musical tinkling and knew it for the destruction of Carcasilla. With a sudden, intolerable vividness he remembered Evaya, and he knew that he had lost.

They dare! They dare to threaten me, of the mighty race of— The name had no meaning even in Alan's altered mind. He had not known until that unspeakable name sounded there that the Alien had taken possession again. But it didn't matter now. He had lost, and he knew it, and the luxury, the bliss of surrender, was creeping warmly along his limbs. Not to fight any longer. Give up the hopeless struggle and let this strange beauty go flooding throughout his brain. This exquisite joy was too great for any human creature to sustain. This passion of hunger must be sated. A thousand years of hunger to be fed in one monstrous draught.

Time stood still, paused, and poised for that draught.

And then—thunder again, and the rainbows of colored agony went raying out around him, colors never seen on earth, spreading circles of pain that loosened the brain in his skull. The veils of darkness withdrew again as the

Alien shuddered and retreated. Alan was aware very dimly that the golden tunnel lay before him.

But he did not see it. He hung submissive in the Alien's grasp. He knew that Sir Colin was staring up at the slope at him, gun lifted, eyes seeking his eyes. He knew when the look of shaken horror dawned upon the old man's face —not horror at defeat, but a deeper revulsion at what Sir Colin saw. . . .

He did not care. He no longer had any capacity to care for anything. He waited for the Alien's return.

And then something stirred far back in his mind, in that corner of the brain which had been the last awareness to go, and now was the first to return.

"Kill it. Kill it. Kill it." Mike Smith was saying, over, and over, in his unmistakable voice.

Alan knew that he was mad. It didn't matter. He did not heed the voices even when Flande's familiar, weary tones spoke above Mike's monotonous chant.

"Yes, you must kill it," said Flande, calmly and sounded far away, though he spoke in the center of Alan's brain. "You must kill it, or I shall never know peace from this savage that is crying for revenge."

A vague point of curiosity quivered in Alan's relaxed mind. He knew they were dead. He had watched them die, long ago and far away.

"What does it matter?" he asked them voicelessly. "Who cares now?"

"I care!" Mike Smith's cry shook the silence.

And Flande said, "For myself, I would not care. I would not lift a finger to help if it meant the lives of all mankind. It does mean that. But I have passed too far beyond to care. If it were not for this—this *thing* bound up with me, because we were transmuted together, I would never speak again. But in this one question he is stronger than I."

"How?" Alan asked incuriously. It didn't matter. He waited only for the Alien to return.

"He was transmuted with one strong desire in his mind," Flande said wearily. "So strong it supersedes all else. The Light-Wearer must die or he will never be still and I shall never know the peace I need. I can crush him out like a candleflame, swallow him up in my own glory, once his desire is sated. But until then—"

Darkness and silence closed down about Alan in one monstrous swoop, a silently roaring vortex of hunger. Anger shook in the depths of it, and scorn. For a moment it stilled the voices in his brain. But then, far back, a point of light began to struggle through the darkness. A sun-circle of light ringed by a corona, and against its burning heart, a double shadow flickering.

Flande said, "Fight it now. Fight it, do you hear! I will help you because I must."

Below his words and running through them Mike's voice cried without inflection, "Kill it. Kill it. Kill it, Drake. Kill it." On and on.

Slowly, reluctantly, Alan felt strength flow back into his stilled mind. He did not want it. He fought against its coming. But Flande was inexorable. And Flande had a power drawn from some inexhaustible source. He was neither man nor god now. He flamed in Alan's mind—a stellar nova, a newborn sun. Alan felt strength pouring irresistibly through his brain. He felt closed doors fly open before that shining flood.

Gunfire thundered all around him, its echoes rolling and redoubling until the world shook with sound. But this time it was not pain. The Alien no longer dwelt in the heart and center of his being. When it withdrew now, shaken and shuddering with the concussion, he blinked unseeing eyes that did not care what they looked upon. But the eyes and the brain behind them were his own again.

This time he was outside the Alien; he would be a stubborn, motionless core about which that vortex would beat in vain when it returned. He knew that passionlessly, not caring.

And the Alien knew it, too. It came back with a suddenness like a tornado's swoop, howling soundlessly with its rage and its ravenous starvation. It was not beaten yet. It fought a double foe, but it had weapons still to fight with . . . weapons tempered for this new, shining enemy filling his victim with its strength.

Alan felt the universe whirl around him. The tunnel was no longer here. The world fell away beneath him. Vertigo more terrible than earthbound man has ever known shook him sickeningly as the ground beneath his feet failed him, and the swimming, impersonal depths of interstellar space spun past his watching eyes, streaked with whirling stars.

Flande shrank a little from the sight. A little. Not enough to matter. Flande had powers to tap now that made earth unnecessary. The Alien raved again with his iron-cold anger, and the deeps of space fell away.

Now they were spinning through the cities of flame, where monstrous citadels floated upon lakes like fire. Beings like the Alien went flashing through their streets, beings unrobed in the light that had veiled them from human gaze.

Alan could not see them. By a strong exertion of his will he *would* not see them. But Flande saw and flinched. Flande still hung on. And the fight went raging on with Alan its voiceless center, the vessel for Flande's dogged strength.

Gunfire again. The Alien gathered itself, shivering, and withdrew. Alan was blind to the tunnel now. He could see nothing but the great corona of light with Flande's image blazoned black upon its surface.

When the Alien came spinning and roaring back, Alan sensed somewhere within its vortex the violence of dawning despair. A subtle weakening of its purpose. But a determination, too, as it dredged up the last terrible power from the bottomless hunger of its being. And the battle took up once more around him.

He did not see the sights that Flande must look upon as the Alien dragged them both reeling through the corridors of its memory. They were sights perceptible only to senses no human owns. That alone saved Alan. If he had seen what Flande saw. . . . But he hung motionless in the heart of the vortex, waiting. Waiting through another burst of gunfire that shook the Alien to its depths.

When it collapsed, the collapse came suddenly. Alan was shocked out of his inertia by the indescribable feeling of surrender in the great tornado that still enveloped him. That terrible, inhuman cyclone had drained itself dry at last. It was running. It was beaten.

So the first of its great race to land upon earth, and the last of that race to live upon earth, knew that it had come to its defeat, its glorious, star-born destiny unfulfilled. And a terrible sorrow shook through the blindness that gripped

Alan. He shared the inhuman grieving of this last of the mighty race whose name mankind would never know—a race with power too vast for man to conceive, with beauty too blinding for man to look upon, with evil grace that struck terror to man's very soul whenever he was obliged to confront it.

In its dying, it fled flashing and shining under-earth, back to the citadel its great kinsmen had reared upon this alien planet. Alan saw it go. He saw the citadel lifting mighty symmetries against the alien moon, doorless, enigmatic, drinking in the pale light of earth.

The citadel had no entrance. But the Alien entered it, and briefly—for the flash of a remembrance—Alan entered, too.

Long ago he had wondered what great halls and mighty, vaulted corridors lay within. He knew now. It had no walls. It had no rooms. The citadel was a solid mass from wall to wall as far as human senses could perceive.

But the Alien went flashing through it along a prescribed course it knew well. Past the memorials of its nameless race that had come and ruled and died. Perhaps past the sepulchres of those who had come after it to earth, and died before its waking. In that one bright journey—in sorrow and loneliness and defeat—it reviewed the history that mankind will never know, and bade good-by to the glories of its mighty kinsmen and its mighty race.

And there in the heart of the citadel which no man will ever enter, the Alien in its own strange way ceased. . . .

"Wake up, laddie!" the burred voice urged. Familiar, from ages ago.

Alan opened his eyes. Glowing walls about him, fiery sun blazing before his face. But there was no shadow upon its surface now. His thoughts paused there, searching back for Flande.

Flande was gone. He had dreamed everything, his shaken mind told him. He must have dreamed it. He looked up to the familiar, ruddy face of the old Scotsman for assurance.

Sir Colin smiled. "We've won, laddie," he said in a thickened voice. "We've done it, somehow! Though for a moment, I thought— Well, no matter now. I saw it go. Och—" His voice softened. "I saw the miracle of *it* going. But I couldna tell you how."

A thin, musical crashing behind him made Alan look over his shoulder. What he saw framed in the tunnel mouth astonished him more than anything that had gone before. Yet it was a simple thing, something he had seen already. It was Flande's tower.

The structure was falling. In the little time while it toppled, then, all this had happened.

He watched it tilt over and down, majestically bowing out above the city. Very slowly it broke in the center and collapsed with a ringing series of crashes as its fragments struck Carcasilla's shining floor very far beneath. Bit by bit the spiral step fell after it.

The noise of its fall went echoing through the city, the vibrations making the delicate suburbs tremble. Here and there, far and near, soaring avenues trembled too much and broke with a singing, vibrant chord like music, and came tinkling and showering down to rouse more echoes, and bring more buildings to lovely, musical ruin.

For the first time since its conception, sound had entered Carcasilla, and sound spelled Carcasilla's doom. Alan stood listening to the delicate, ringing chords of the collapsing buildings. He was thinking of Evaya. He knew that he had won now, and that somewhere along the Way of the Gods, perhaps coming nearer and nearer with every passing moment, the real Evaya would be moving. Evaya with life glowing again like a lighted lamp behind her features as exquisite as carved ivory. Her hair lifting and floating upon the darkened air.

Evaya, coming back to ruined Carcasilla.

Yes, he had won. And he had lost. Mankind was reprieved now. The Source of the fountain that made Carcasilla immortal would go out to Venus in the waiting ship, and Sir Colin would go with it! Sir Colin, and Karen, and the Terasi. There would be a green world again, fragrant and sweet, shining with dew and rain.

But he would never see it. He would wait here for Evaya, who could not go. He would wait with her, here in shattered Carcasilla, while immortality ran low in the dying fountain and darkness closed in forever upon Earth.

* * *

Sir Colin nibbled thoughtfully at his fantastically featured pen. Then he dipped the quill into ink crushed from berries that never sprang from the sod of earth, and wrote on.

"—so we left them there," he wrote. "And because the journey was so long, and I growing old, I misdoubt I shall ever know their fate. But I know Alan Drake, and I know what happened to him. At least, in part I know—in his long fight with the Alien that lasted only while I fired five shots as fast as I could pull the trigger. He told me what he could of it. He told me about Flande, opening bright doors in his brain to the light of that burning sun.

"Such a light made Flande a demigod. Alan Drake had none so much of it, but a little taste he had. And I believe that taste was enough. I believe, as sure as there was a Scotland, that mankind still lives upon Old Earth.

"If any man could keep it alive, the man is Alan Drake. I make this record for the new generation of Terasi to remember, and for their children and grandchildren.

"Some day, somehow, I swear to you—your cousins from Old Earth will make their voices heard on Venus. And they will speak the name of Drake.

"The thing we left for them should be a legend by the time your generation reads this record. You will have heard of the shining room we took our Power-Source from, and how the stones glowed on after it was gone. It had poured out energy so long into those walls that energy still lived in them, and I think must live on—long enough.

"Long enough to power the machines they'll need —those fragile-seeming Carcasillians who were built on a tougher framework than anyone knew unless—as Alan knew—one had occasion to find out! He would never have spoken to me of the steely, resilient strength of Evaya's body when he held her in his arms, had he not known how important that knowledge would be to the future of mankind on Old Earth.

"So we know the Carcasillians were strong. And we know they had a limited source of power to set their machines going in the caverns the Terasi left behind. And we know, too, something we were too blind to think of at the time. There is one power-source upon Old Earth still living and strong in her extreme age. The great tides that thunder around the planet, following the moon, carving a mighty gorge in the earth as they race on. If the Carcasillians with their machines and their resilient strength can harness that tide—who knows, Old Earth may yet shine green again in the heavens!

"It is my belief they can. It is my belief that Alan Drake, with his knowledge and his power bequeathed by Flande, can save his beloved and the people of his beloved, and the world on which he chose to stay, because his beloved had to remain there.

"The fountain of immortality died, and Carcasillians live on. I shall believe it until I die myself. And, one day, I believe, all Venus will hear the great story which I can only guess at now. The story I shall never know."

WINNER OF THE HUGO AWARD AND THE NEBULA AWARD FOR BEST SCIENCE FICTION NOVEL OF THE YEAR

*04594	Babel 17 Delany $1.50
*05476	Best Science Fiction of the Year Del Rey $1.25
06218	The Big Time Leiber $1.25
*10623	City Simak $1.75
16649	The Dragon Masters Vance $1.50
16704	Dream Master Zelazny $1.50
19683	The Einstein Intersection Delany $1.50
24903	Four For Tomorrow Zelazny $1.50
47071	The Last Castle Vance 95¢
47803	Left Hand of Darkness Leguin $1.95
72784	Rite of Passage Panshin $1.50
79173	Swords and Deviltry Leiber $1.50
80694	This Immortal Zelazny $1.50

Available wherever paperbacks are sold or use this coupon.

ace books, (Dept. MM) Box 576, Times Square Station
New York, N.Y. 10036
Please send me titles checked above.

I enclose $.............. Add 35c handling fee per copy.

Name ....

Address ....

City.................... State.............. Zip........

*01570	**Alien Planet** Pratt	75¢
*02938	**Armageddon 2419 A.D.** Nowlan	$1.25
06713	**The Blind Spot** Hall & Flint	$1.50
07690	**The Brain-Stealers** Leinster	$1.50
07840	**A Brand New World** Cummings	$1.25
27291	**The Galaxy Primes** Smith	$1.25
52831	**Metropolis** Von Harbou	$1.25
53870	**The Moon Is Hell** Campbell	95¢
70301	**The Radio Beasts** Farley	$1.50
70320	**The Radio Planet** Farley	$1.50
75431	**Science Fiction—The Great Years Part II** Pohl	$1.50
75894	**Sentinels from Space** Russell	$1.50
*84331	**The Ultimate Weapon** Campbell	$1.25
87182	**War Against the Rull** Van Vogt	$1.50

Available wherever paperbacks are sold or use this coupon.

ace books, (Dept. MM) Box 576, Times Square Station
New York, N.Y. 10036

Please send me titles checked above.

I enclose $.................. Add 35c handling fee per copy.

Name ....

Address ....

City................:....... State.............. Zip.........

45C

ACE SCIENCE FICTION SPECIALS

10150 **Challenge The Hellmaker**
Richmond $1.25

20660 **Endless Voyage** Bradley $1.25

21430 **Equality in the Year 2000**
Reynolds $1.50

25461 **From the Legend of Biel**
Staton $1.50

30420 **Growing Up In the Tier 3000**
Gotschalk $1.25

37171 **The Invincible** Lem $1.50

46850 **Lady of the Bees** Swann $1.25

66780 **A Plague of All Cowards**
Barton $1.50

71160 **Red Tide** Chapman & Tarzan
$1.25

81900 **Tournement of Thorns**
Swann $1.50

Available wherever paperbacks are sold or use this coupon.

ace books, (Dept. MM) Box 576, Times Square Station
New York, N.Y. 10036

Please send me titles checked above.

I enclose $.................. Add 35c handling fee per copy.

Name ....

Address ....

City.................... State............. Zip........

64B

SAMUEL R. DELANY

*04594 Babel 17 $1.50

19683 Einstein Intersection $1.50

20571 The Ballad of Beta2/Empire Star $1.25

22642 The Fall of the Towers $1.95

39021 Jewels of Aptor 75¢

ROGER ZELAZNY

37468 Isle of the Dead $1.50

16704 The Dream Master $1.50

24903 Four For Tomorrow $1.50

80694 This Immortal $1.50

PHILIP JOSÉ FARMER

05360 Behind the Walls of Terra $1.25

78652 The Stone God Awakens $1.25

89238 The Wind Whales of Ishmael $1.25

Available wherever paperbacks are sold or use this coupon.

ace books, (Dept. MM) Box 576. Times Square Station
New York. N.Y. 10036

Please send me titles checked above.

I enclose $................ Add 35c handling fee per copy.

Name ....

Address ....

City...................... State.............. Zip........

44F

CLIFFORD D. SIMAK

10624	**City**	$1.75
77220	**So Bright the Vision**	$1.50
81002	**Time and Again**	$1.75
82442	**The Trouble With Tycho**	$1.50

Available wherever paperbacks are sold or use this coupon.

ace books, (Dept. MM) Box 576, Times Square Station
New York, N.Y. 10036

Please send me titles checked above.

I enclose $................ Add 35c handling fee per copy.

Name ....

Address ....

City.................... State............. Zip........

34C

THE CLASSIC SEQUEL TO THE SCIENCE FICTION BESTSELLER—*LITTLE FUZZY!*

Too long out of print, these delightful SF classics are finally available to the legions of readers waiting to discover the new human race — Fuzzy Sapiens!

Available wherever paperbacks are sold or use this coupon.

ace books, (Dept. MM) Box 576, Times Square Station New York. N.Y. 10036

Please send me _____ copies of LITTLE FUZZY @ $1.25 & _____ copies of FUZZY SAPIENS @ $1.50 each. I enclose $_____. Add 35c handling fee per copy.

Name ....

Address ....

City...................... State............. Zip........